The Dead Whisper

Emma Clapperton

Also by Emma Clapperton

Beyond Evidence

Available in ebook only, a free novella

The Suicide Plan

Praise For Beyond Evidence

'For a debut novel this was a very good book. It is quite pacey, with realistic characters and dialogue, twists and turns and ongoing suspense.'

Joseph Calleja – Relax And Read Reviews

'I really enjoyed reading this book. It combined murder, mystery and a bit of paranormal activity to keep me on the edge of my seat.'

Noelle Holten – Crimebookjunkie

'The book moves along at a steady pace with suspense all the way through that keeps the reader turning the pages.'

Jill Burkinshaw – Books n All

'This is certainly a page turner I read it in one afternoon the author grabs you from start and keeps you there until the very last page.'

Shell Baker – Chelle's Book Reviews

'Beyond Evidence is a wonderful crime/thriller story with a paranormal twist.'

Clair Boor – Have Books Will Read

'There are some very shocking discoveries in this story that just give it plenty OMG moments as more of the story unfolds and it all becomes a race against time and very personal.'

Susan Hampson – Books from Dusk Till Dawn

This book is dedicated to
Alexander and Elaine Clapperton.

Prologue

3 May 1950

Standing by her husband as he watched his father's coffin being lowered into the ground broke her heart. Anna Henderson wept softly as she watched the man she loved so dearly fight for composure. No matter what age you were, it was never easy saying goodbye to a parent. Anna knew this time around was going to be the hardest for George, for they had only just buried Edith, shortly before Walter's passing.

Edith and Walter Henderson were George's late parents, and a fine job they had made of it. Their son was a gentleman and a credit to his parents. Having been brought up in a house that had been big enough to host an army, George was not at all spoiled or selfish. He would give his last penny to anyone who was in desperate need of it. Anna remembered the stories George had told her about his father, Walter, and how he had taught him about the value of money, how the hard-working man should always bring the family together around the dinner table. She loved that about him, how George had always lived his life by that rule, and it had never let him down. Walter had shown George the importance of the women in their lives, and how without them, nothing would be worth working towards. Men like this were rare, as far as Edith had been concerned, and she had been immensely proud her only son had turned out like his father.

Anna, too, was entirely proud to say that she was married to a wonderful man who had come from a wonderful family. The Henderson men came from a long line of hard-workers, and nothing was ever taken for granted. She loved the history of the Henderson family, and that she would be part of that history one day. That, hopefully, in years to come, her great-great-grandchildren would sit around the dinner table and listen to stories of the ancestors from years gone by.

***

Looking down at his father's coffin, George thought back to when he learned about his bloodline. He remembered listening to the story of the Hendersons and felt the corners of his mouth raise a little.

"I was fortunate to inherit the manor and the whisky business from my old man. I knew it would be hard work to keep up the success, but I wasn't opposed to the challenge." Walter had told him.

"How long has the whisky distillery been going for?" George asked.

"It's hard to say. My old man could only go so far back in the trail, but from my understanding, it's been on the go from as far back as the early 1800s."

"That's impressive."

"Aye, it is indeed. I remember the day he told me it would all be mine. On my twenty-first birthday, it was. Best present I could have ever asked for. But it wasn't something I was to take lightly. I had to earn my keep, earn my old man's trust that I would work at keeping the business going. I worked the floor, producing the product itself. I can remember just standing back and taking a deep breath, allowing the whisky's scent to filter through me. I loved that smell; it made me imagine my future. I'll never forget that feeling."

"Must have been a wonderful feeling," George replied.

"It was. And you will feel the same when your time comes, when I'm gone."

George watched his family and friends around him as they grieved for his father. He had been a well-respected man, one who had made many friends and acquaintances over the years. George felt his wife squeeze his hand, and it brought back the harsh reality that he would never hear Walter's voice again, never see his gentle smile, or hear his larger-than-life laugh.

"It'll be okay. He's in a better place," whispered Anna.

George nodded. "I know he is. It just doesn't seem right. How am I supposed to go on, knowing he won't be there, if I need him? Or if I have a question about the business…he won't be there to answer me."

"You'll have all of the answers, darling, you will. All you have to do is think of him, and they will come to you."

George wasn't so sure. He felt lost without Walter, who had been George's guidance in life.

"We commit Walter's body to the ground, ashes to ashes, dust to dust," the priest spoke, his voice low but ever present. Someone offered a box with dirt inside for George to throw in the first handful. He grabbed a fistful and squeezed as hard as he could, but for some reason, he didn't want to let go.

"Go on, George," he heard Anna prompt.

"I can't."

"You can. You're a Henderson."

George took a deep breath, desperately trying to keep the tears at bay, before he released his fist and let the dirt fall gently on top of Walter's coffin.

He was briefly aware Anna was repeating the process, along with a few other family members, before George collapsed to his knees in despair.

The piper played 'Amazing Grace' as the crowd made their way back into the house. George stayed down on his knees, silently thanking everyone as they gave him the space that he needed. He was grateful for Anna, who stayed by his side, allowing him to expel his anguish.

The springtime breeze was barely warm, and the air carried a dampness which matched the circumstances of the day. George felt Anna's hand fall upon his shoulder. "I'll give you a moment, dear."

He held his breath as he listened to the gentle wind, hoping to hear his father's voice, but, of course, all he heard was the breeze brushing through the tall fir trees around the grounds of Henderson Manor.

"What am I supposed to do with all of this without you?" George asked out loud. He waited for an answer, willing for a sign to come and reassure him. Nothing came.

George stood up and brushed himself off. He gathered his emotions, displayed composure once more, and made his way back towards the house.

He looked in through the kitchen door and could see Anna busying herself with trays of glasses for the people who had come to pay their respects. Of course, the family had hired help for the occasion, but he knew it was Anna's way of coping with the situation. George made his way into the large kitchen, expecting Anna to fuss around him, like she always did. However, this time, she just smiled at him and carried on with what she was doing. She was in and out of the kitchen like a woman possessed, although she carried herself like a calm breeze. She had such a gentle manner about her that even when she was angry about something, she was as polite as one could be when angry.

"Take as much time out as you need, dear," she said as she poured a large brandy for him.

"Actually, would you mind pouring a whisky? If I'm going to celebrate my father's life, I may as well do it with his own brand."

Anna smiled, but it didn't reach her eyes. "How silly of me, of course."

George led Anna by the hand, out to the rear grounds of the house where the family plot had just received its second member. He put his arm around Anna's shoulder and raised the other hand, holding a glass of the family brand of Henderson Whisky.

"Here's to you, Dad. I hope you find Mum, and your broken heart is finally mended. Cheers." George threw the whisky down his throat and placed the glass next to the many wreaths and flowers that people had left in respect. The plot was still to be filled in.

"Let's go inside, darling," George said.

"Are you ready to face everyone? You don't need more time?"

"I have everything I need inside that house. Let's go."

1

Glasgow Royal Concert Hall was packed out for the third night in a row, and Sam Leonard felt excited at the success but relief it was finally over. He had worked on his performance for months, and now the show had come to a close, he felt like he could finally relax. It was his first stage production where he played the lead role, and he had been so nervous just thinking about it. The venue could hold 1200 people, and as he stood on the stage, he could see not one empty seat on any of the three nights.

His role in the play was a husband struggling with alcoholism and a failing marriage to a woman with cancer. Sam had hesitated when offered the part at first, not sure if his experience as an actor would be enough to fulfil the role. His agent had encouraged him that he was perfect for the part, and so, after some persuasion, he signed the contract and began rehearsing.

It all seemed to speed by, and as the curtain rose for the final bow, Sam focused on the back of the audience. Lights flashed from the cameras in the audience, and his ears buzzed from the sounds of cheers and applause.

The curtain was lowered, and the rest of the cast applauded one another for their hard work and commitment to the play.

"Well done, Sam. You were fantastic, yet again," said his agent, Miles.

"Thanks. I'm overwhelmed by the response!"

"You should be. They bloody love you out there."

"Oh, I don't know about that."

"Are you kidding? This play is going to make you huge!" Miles patted him on the shoulder.

"Cheers, Miles. I'm going to get changed. You joining us for dinner and drinks?" he asked, motioning a glance to the other cast members.

"Need you ask?" Miles replied, with a bright, wide grin.

Sam made his way back to his dressing room and went into the shower. He turned the switch to power mode and stood under the head, allowing the water to beat down on his neck and shoulders. He hadn't realised it, but in the last three nights, his neck and shoulder muscles had been so tense that as soon as the curtain fell for the last time, he felt the pounding headache set in.

He finished showering, stepped out of the cubicle, and reached for his sports bag. Sam pulled out the paracetamol and swallowed two with a large glass of water.

As he pulled on his jeans and a shirt, he heard a knock at the dressing room door. "Come in!"

"You ready yet, Mr Diva?" Miles laughed.

Sam rolled his eyes and smiled. "Diva? As if, mate."

They made their way down Sauchiehall Street and were the last to arrive out of the cast and crew from the play. They had hired out three booths in a bar called 'Lounge' and had pre-ordered food and drinks.

A few hours passed, and the Lounge bar was getting busy. Sam had relaxed, and his headache had subsided. He stood at the bar waiting to order a drink and couldn't help feeling eyes on him. He turned to see a young woman standing behind him. She smiled, and he returned the smile.

"Hi," she said. Her voice was soft.

"Hi," Sam replied.

"You're Sam Leonard, aren't you?"

"That's me, and your name is?"

Her smile widened. "It's Deborah."

***

Deborah Bell stood talking to Sam, and her entire body felt like one huge thudding heart. She tried to control the quiver in her voice, and she didn't have to strain to hear the blood rushing through her ears.

Deborah Bell was twenty-five, and her blonde hair sat on her shoulders. Sam was almost a whole head and shoulders taller than she was, and this made her feel even more nervous. She was Sam's biggest fan, and she found it difficult to keep that information under control.

"Would you like a drink?" Sam asked.

"Thanks, I'll have a vodka with lime, please."

As Sam turned to order the drinks, Deborah stood behind him and tried to compose herself. She had never had the guts to actually approach him before, but her determination to meet him just once pushed her to do it that night. She wished her heart would calm down as it was banging so hard against her chest, and she was sure that if in a quiet room, even he would hear it.

She had watched Sam for a long time on television and had been to all of the plays he had appeared in. She always knew what his next job was and where he would be appearing. She admired his work, followed his acting career and, most of all, thought he was the most beautiful man ever to have been created.

She reminded herself to play it cool; if he learned how much she knew of him, what she had gone through to be near him, it might scare him off. But all she wanted was to have a drink with him.

He turned to face her, passing her the glass as he did so. "So, what are you up to tonight?"

Shit! I didn't think this through. She searched her brain for a quick answer. "My friends are upstairs. I wanted a drink, but the bar upstairs is too busy, so I thought I would chance using this one. Oh, thanks by the way." She held up the drink. *Nice one.*

"Am I keeping you?" he asked.

"Not at all, most of their boyfriends are here, so to be honest, you're keeping me from feeling like a bit of a spare part."

"Oh, right, your boyfriend not here tonight, then?"

Deborah's stomach flipped, and she had to contain the giggle that crept up from her throat. "I don't have one, actually."

"No? You'll be able to join me for more drinks, then."

Deborah sensed this wasn't a question. "Why not?" she replied, trying not to sound too excited.

Her fingers tingled as he took her hand in his and led her away from the bar towards a more secluded area of the room.

Deborah's heart raced, and the more time she spent with him, the more she became attracted to him. "You don't want to join your friends?" she asked.

"Not really. I've spent the last eight months with them, day in and day out. A few hours without them won't kill me." He smiled.

Deborah slid into the booth and sat beside him. She was close enough she could smell his scent. Close enough she could hear his breath, had the music not been so loud. Close enough it drove her crazy not to touch him. *I don't know how much faster my heart can beat before it explodes.*

"So, tell me about yourself," Sam said.

Deborah felt lost for words and couldn't suppress the smile that was beginning to make her cheeks ache. "I'm at university."

"What are you studying?"

"A degree in journalism."

"Cool. Are you nearly finished?"

"Actually, I'm doing a placement at the moment," she said. She questioned whether or not she should reveal where the placement was, and that she had asked her lecturer if she could go to that particular venue.

"Locally?" he asked, seeming oblivious to her nerves.

She decided not to tell him yet. "I'm in a local newspaper office. It's small, and nothing exciting happens, really."

He was nodding as she spoke, as if enjoying the conversation. There were a few moments where he stared into her eyes. Again, her heart raced, and now, all she wanted was to kiss him.

"So, you're an actor?" She broke the silence, maintaining her self-control.

"That I am. Have you seen any of my stuff?" he asked.

"Just the play tonight," she lied. Of course she was aware of everything he had worked on: television adverts, television dramas, newspaper articles, magazine, and radio interviews. She had even followed him to the venues where he worked on all of those things, but thankfully, he had never come across her. If he had, they wouldn't be sitting together.

"Oh, you were in the theatre? What did you think?" His eyes lit up.

"You were very good. You play a good drunk," she said, with a smile.

What she really wanted to say was she thought he was amazing, and if love at first sight was real, then she was very much in love with him. Deborah knew what she was feeling for Sam Leonard was not normal, but the lust to have him and the uncontrollable desire within to keep him near her was becoming unbearable.

"So, what do you say we go somewhere quieter?" He leaned in close to her face.

"Where do you have in mind?" she asked. She wanted to tell him exactly how she felt, but she knew it could destroy any chance she had of being with him.

There's no need to tell him. You have him right now, and that's all you have ever wanted. Just take what's here and enjoy it, she thought.

"What about going back to my place?" he asked.

"Sounds like a good idea to me."

They slid out of the booth, and Sam took her hand and led her down to the street. It was cold outside, and Sam commented on Deborah's goose bumps on her arms. The little blonde hairs stood on end, and she trembled in the November breeze.

"Here, you can have my jacket," Sam said, wrapping it around her. As his fingers gently brushed off her shoulder, she felt the urge to kiss him, but she fought it off. She couldn't believe she was going to spend the night in Sam Leonard's flat.

A taxi pulled up outside the Lounge bar, and Sam opened the door to let Deborah in. As it pulled away, she could feel every pulse in her body thumping, could hear the blood rushing in her ears. She knew she should have had another vodka to stay calm, but when he had offered to take her back to his flat, she just wanted to get out of the bar and into a taxi as fast as her legs would carry her.

"So, do you live far?" she asked, trying to take her mind off what was about to happen between them.

"I'm only in Merchant City and not far in, either. We will be there in about five minutes."

The taxi pulled up outside a set of new build flats, and Deborah didn't have time to look around the street as she was gently but quickly being led up the four flights of stairs to Sam's flat.

"Do you live by yourself?" she asked.

"No, my flatmate is out 'til tomorrow," he replied as he put his key in the door.

He allowed Deborah to go in first, and as she looked around, she couldn't quite believe she was in Sam Leonard's home. It was so clean and tidy, with photographs on the wall of friends and maybe family; she wasn't entirely sure. He guided her into the kitchen, and she sat down on a barstool.

"Drink?" Sam asked as he opened the fridge and pulled out a bottle of wine.

"Yes, please," Deborah replied, noticing a gentle quiver in her voice.

He poured a large glass and handed it to her, again his fingers brushing her hand as she received the glass. She almost felt an electrical charge run through her fingers at his touch. As he turned to get himself a glass, she gulped the large glass of rosé wine down and felt it burn in her chest.

He turned and walked towards her, and she felt her body tingle. "So, how long have you lived here, then?"

"About a year," he replied.

Now their faces were close together, she could feel his breath on her face, and it smelled good.

"You smell great," he said as their noses brushed together.

"Thank you. So do you." She noticed she was whispering.

He took a sip of wine from his glass.

"I don't normally do this, you know," Deborah said, with a gentle smile.

"What's that?"

"Come back to a guy's flat who I've only just met."

"Why make the exception for me?" he asked, pushing his lips to meet hers but ensuring there was still a few millimetres between them.

"I don't know," she whispered again.

She could not be sure who started the kiss, but at that point in time, she did not care. It was gentle at first, tender, in fact. But as the kiss lasted, she felt Sam push hard on her lips, and his tongue gently search for hers.

If lust could create electricity, then Deborah would have enough to generate power to Sam's flat for a month. She felt weak under the passion in his kiss, and he took control of her.

He slid his hand under her thighs and lifted her from the barstool. She closed her eyes and allowed him to carry her to another room, what she assumed was the bedroom.

He laid her down on his bed and gently pushed down on top of her. He was heavy, but she liked the feeling of him on her. He pulled his shirt over his head with one hand and with the other, gently unbuttoned her blouse. He opened it wide, and she slid her arms out.

Deborah pulled at Sam's belt. His thumb crept through the space between her skin and underwear, pulling the material downward.

Deborah relished every second with Sam, taking in every part of his body as they spent the night together.

As Sam slept, Deborah familiarized herself with his home, looking at photographs on the walls and memorizing everything around her. There was nothing she could not know about Sam Leonard.

2

Jenny Lawson was sitting at the breakfast bar in the flat she shared with Sam. She skimmed through the newspaper as she sipped at her mug of black tea. She had heard Sam getting up earlier, and he had been in the shower for around thirty minutes. As he entered the kitchen, he saw the large grin Jenny had on her face.

"What are you so smiley about this morning?" he asked her as he pulled a box of cereal out from the cupboard.

"Shouldn't I be asking you that question?" She pointed to the small black handbag that was sitting on the counter. "So, she didn't fancy staying all night?"

"I guess not. When I woke up, she was gone, but I'm glad. I can't be bothered with the small talk once the alcohol has worn off and the sex has been had," he said smugly.

"Oh, you dirty stop out!" Jenny laughed. "She may have left, but she clearly wants to see you again, because she left a note with her number on it."

Jenny and Sam had been best friends since they were in high school and had never been anything more. A lot of people had asked them if they had ever kissed, or wanted to try it. Their answer had always been the same. 'Would you kiss your best friend if you didn't fancy them?'

They had decided to live together when they were at college, and the setup was still working, so they had decided to keep living together until the day one of them was ready to move on to somewhere else.

"What do you think I should do?" Sam held up the handbag.

"If I were her, I would want you to phone me."

"Really?"

"Yep, the way I see it is, she gets her bag back, and you'll know if you want to see her again."

"How do you work that one out?" Sam asked.

"You'll see her for the first time sober, and you'll know if she's as good looking as you thought she was last night."

Sam smiled and gave Jenny a pat on the head. "You know me so well."

"Yes, I do," she replied, with a smile.

Jenny noticed how quiet Sam was while he ate breakfast, and she wondered if he was thinking about the girl. Unless he told her, she never could tell what went on in his head. Jenny watched him leave the kitchen and heard him making his way between bedroom and bathroom. She eyed the handbag again and wondered who the girl was.

A few minutes later, he popped his head around the kitchen door. "See you sometime this afternoon? Maybe we could meet up for a drink and lunch?"

"Sounds like a plan. Text me when you decide where we're going, and I'll meet you there," Jenny replied as she got up to fill the dishwasher.

"Will do," he said, making his way to the front door. Jenny heard it close behind him.

Jenny pressed the button that was labelled 'Intense wash' and left the kitchen to go and get ready for the day.

On her way past Sam's bedroom, she paused when she saw the door was open. He had actually managed to make the bed. *Jeez, he must be in a good mood,* Jenny thought as she closed the door.

The flat was always quiet when Sam was not around. She did not like being on her own because the place gave her shivers, but she never really understood why. The flats in Merchant City were relatively new, so there wasn't much chance that it was haunted, if you believed in that sort of thing, of course.

Jenny and Sam's flat was decorated according to each of their individual tastes. It was modern and fresh, with white and slate grey painted walls and wooden flooring. There were photo frames on the walls all around the flat, and there were also frames that included photographs of Sam's achievements, like the cast on the last night of a sell-out show. There were also posters of his shows and appearances up on the walls of his bedroom.

Perhaps this made Sam look a little vain, although apart from the frames, Sam never came across as such. He kept himself to himself generally and tried not to be noticed when out on his daily business. He was quite well known in Scotland, and not a day went by where someone did *not* notice him.

***

Staring down at the phone as it rang, her heart raced so much she began to feel sick. Not wanting to miss the call, she lifted the phone and answered it. "Hello?"

"Hello, Deborah? It's Sam here."

"Oh, hello again." She bit her bottom lip, stunned he had actually called and so soon after she had left.

"You left your bag here last night."

"Oh, really? I thought I'd left it in the taxi that dropped me home."

"Would you like it back?"

Deborah sensed he was teasing her. She liked it. Deborah hesitated; she really was pleased to hear from him, but she was not at all prepared for the call to have come so soon. "Yes, I would," she replied, trying to sound as equally teasing as Sam had.

"So, should we meet up?" Sam asked.

"Yes, that would be good."

Is he asking me on a date, or does he just want to hand my bag back?

"Let me take you out again, properly this time." He answered her silent question.

Deborah tried to control her breathing, but felt it impossible. "Okay, where do you want to go?" *God, even his voice is beautiful. Is this really happening?*

"I'll take you somewhere special." He was speaking so low, it was almost a whisper. "A romantic dinner, wine, and maybe back to mine for afters?"

"Sounds good." Her throat had become dry. She found herself clinging to the phone as though it were the most precious thing she owned.

"Great. I'll pick you up at seven tonight."

Deborah's heart fluttered, and she panicked. "No, we can meet in town."

"You don't want me to pick you up?"

"No, I'll meet you. You could be an axe murderer, for all I know. I don't want you knowing where I live."

"Good move, Miss Bell. I'll meet you at seven at the new Italian restaurant on Argyle Street."

"Okay, sounds great. See you tonight, Mr Leonard."

They hung up, and Deborah noticed she had backed herself onto the wall in her bedroom as she spoke to Sam. She peeled herself off the wall and made her way into the bathroom.

As she thought about the man of her dreams, she wondered if seeing him again was such a good idea. She couldn't pretend to know nothing about him, could she? Obviously being a fan and then becoming the date wouldn't be easy to do, but she was living her dream, so why not?

She knew she had to, but her big secret wasn't far from the back of her mind. She had followed Sam's career for the last three years and watched him become a Scottish star.

Deborah knew everything there was to know about Sam Leonard: his career to-date, the shows, the television appearances, radio interviews, past girlfriends, everything. It was her knowledge on his previous relationship she had to keep quiet.

If she was going to go on this date, it might turn into something serious. She asked herself if she was prepared to deal with a relationship with such a high-profile man. She might become high profile herself, and if she did, she would have so much explaining to do, to a lot of people.

Deborah put that thought to the back of her mind and decided to enjoy the moments that were to come.

3

Sam walked into the café, and if he wasn't hungry before then, he was now. He loved the smell of fresh bread and coffee, and that was the scent invading his nostrils as soon as he was inside the door. He looked for a table and sat down as a waitress approached him. "You're Sam Leonard, aren't you?"

Oh, here we go, he sighed inwardly. "Yes, that's me."

The girl blushed a shade of crimson and handed Sam the lunch menu. "Uh, erm, if you need anything at all, just ask. My name is Claire."

"Thanks, Claire." He took the menu from her, careful not to make skin to skin contact. "I'll decide what I'm having once my friend arrives."

Claire, the waitress, scurried back to the counter as Jenny walked through the doorway.

The sound of teacups clinking on saucers and coffee machines hissing made Sam feel relaxed. The café was empty, except for the waitress, which he was glad for. The surroundings were decorated a mocha colour, with leather couches at the waiting area next to the door. There were picture frames all around the place with fifties-style photographs inside them.

"Sorry I'm late; I got side-tracked," Jenny said as she sat down, fighting with shopping bags which refused to go under the table.

"By a shoe sale, no doubt?"

"Ha, you know me so well. Fifty percent off, so I bought two pairs."

Sam rolled his eyes and raised his hand to alert the waitress. She was at the table in an instant and had an expectant smile across her face. "Yes, Sam, what can I get you?"

Jenny looked at her, then to Sam with a confused expression across her face.

"I'll have a chocolate cappuccino, and Jenny will have..."

Jenny still appeared confused. "Erm, I'll have a black tea please."

Claire didn't make eye contact with Jenny as she spoke. She only watched Sam and continued to stand at the table after they had given their order, almost in a trance.

"That'll be all," Jenny said, with a little force.

Claire snapped out of her trance and blushed a shade of crimson again. "Oh, yes, sorry. I'll be right with you."

Sam laughed quietly and shook his head as Claire walked away from their table.

"Do you know her?" Jenny asked.

"No." Sam was still laughing gently.

"So, how?"

"A fan, most likely. I don't know. She asked me if I was Sam Leonard, and when I said yes, she went all weird."

Jenny laughed. "I can't take you anywhere. So, how did it go with...Deborah, is it?"

"Actually, I asked her out again," Sam replied, aware he was being watched from the counter by the star-struck waitress.

Jenny followed Sam's gaze and caught Claire's eye, and again, her skin had become red and blotchy through a mixture of embarrassment and excitement.

"What is *with* her? You'd think that she'd never met a famous person before."

Sam frowned. "I'm hardly famous, Jenny."

"She seems to see it that way. I mean, look at her. She can't take her eyes off you!" Jenny raised her voice.

Sam cringed. "What are you doing?"

"What? She needs to tone it down and stop making you uncomfortable."

Sam wasn't sure how to take that. He knew Jenny was looking out for him, but for Christ sake, she didn't have to do it like this.

"Jenny, it's fine, honestly. She's just a little shy. Wouldn't you be, if you were in the presence of someone famous?" he said, using his fingers to make inverted commas.

Jenny sat back in her seat and took a silent, deep breath. Sam looked up at Claire, who had turned her back to their table.

Sam knew Jenny was protective of him, especially since the incident from a few months earlier. "Jenny, it's okay. We're having lunch. It's all cool, nothing's wrong here."

"I know. I just don't want you-know-what to happen again."

Sam smiled gently. Jenny had been his rock when it had all gone wrong. He knew in his mind it was unlikely to happen again, and Jenny probably did, too, but sometimes when it crossed his mind, he couldn't help but worry. "Hey, as long as you're around, I don't think I've anything to worry about. And don't you go getting all worried for me. I'm a big boy, Jenny. I can handle things on my own."

Jenny seemed to relax at his comment. "I know you can. You know what I'm like, and I couldn't bear to see you go through that again."

"And I won't. I ended it for a reason, and I haven't heard from her since. It's all fine now—she's gone."

A few silent moments passed before Claire returned to the table with their order. She smiled gently at Jenny, who returned the smile but only briefly. "I'm sorry if I made you uncomfortable, Mr Leonard. I didn't mean to," Claire said quietly.

"You didn't. Thanks." He felt sorry for the waitress. The poor girl was only doing her job. He didn't want Jenny thinking of every female the way she thought about *her*.

'Her' was an ex, sort of. Sam had gone on a few dates with her, and they had become an item. Zoe was her name, and a nice girl she was, too…at first.

Zoe had learned about Sam's fame (Sam didn't believe he was famous, just that he was successful in his work as an actor) after the first date. He had chosen to tell her, knowing the new relationship could go one of two ways: intense or on course as normal.

At first, it seemed to flow as a new relationship would. They went on dates, talked and dined, all the normal stuff. After a few weeks, Sam was really beginning to like Zoe and decided he wanted to make them an official couple.

That was when things had started to go wrong. Zoe changed. She hated the fact he lived with Jenny, even though she would never admit it. He did tell her there was nothing to worry about, and that he and Jenny were just friends, but Zoe would always go quiet around Jenny. Sam couldn't cope with his best friend and his girlfriend not getting on well, so he made a decision. He would only see Zoe without Jenny's company for a while, to see how it worked.

It didn't work well. Sam received threatening notes through his door, which said things like Jenny would be harmed if she didn't stay away from Sam. He and Jenny would also receive threatening text messages from an unknown number and silent phone calls, all, of course, when Zoe wasn't with Sam.

Sam never could be one hundred percent sure, but his instinct told him his every move was being watched, followed, and listened to. He had the prickling feeling on his back whenever he was alone, and as the weeks drew on, he decided to confront who he believed to be behind it all: Zoe.

Sam had distanced himself from her in the time the threats and stalker-like behaviour had begun. He hadn't bothered to tell her why, but he was pretty sure she would know the reason. But she still incessantly called and turned up to the flat. He was glad Jenny had been there to help him; she was able to put sympathy into her tone and make it look as though she understood she missed Sam but gently tell her he was no longer interested.

Sam had thought Jenny's words had done the trick, but he still felt uneasy. He still received disturbing letters which threatened violence, and his phone rang for the majority of the day and into the night. The threats on Jenny became more violent and intense.

Enough is enough, Sam had thought. He had decided to turn up at her house, unannounced. If he was going to find out about her unnecessary behaviour towards him, then he didn't want to do it with a warning. He also wanted to scare her shitless so she would leave him and Jenny alone.

As he had approached Zoe's house, he wondered why it had come to this so suddenly. She had been lovely to begin with and then taken an instant dislike to Jenny. In fact, dislike was too kind a word. Hatred would be more fitting, even though Jenny had done nothing to cause it. You could hardly say being a friend of Sam's was an excuse.

Maybe it was due to them living together, and Zoe had become intensely jealous. It was the only explanation Sam could think of. Whatever the reason, he had to find out why and tell her to back off. He walked up the gravel driveway with his jacket slung over his shoulder. He was surprised to see Zoe had opened the door before he'd even thought about knocking on it.

"Didn't expect to see you here," she said, with a timid voice.

"No? I didn't expect you to turn out psychotic, but we learn something new every day, don't we?" Sam's reply was nastier than he had first anticipated.

She stood firmly in the doorway, not granting access to the hall. "You want to talk?"

"You're damn right I do, although I'll be doing the talking, and you'll be doing the listening."

Zoe nodded and stood back, allowing Sam to enter. He hesitated at first, unsure of how she would react when he was inside. "You're not going to go all possessive and lock me in, are you?"

Zoe's expression was sad, with a deep sense of loss reflecting in her eyes. "Of course not. I would never hurt anyone, Sam, let alone you."

Sam watched as Zoe closed the door on the world outside, and he genuinely wondered if he would ever see the other side of it again.

She led him into the sitting room, where she gestured for him to sit down. A large rocking chair sat in the corner next to the bay window, and an old grandfather clock stood in the opposite corner. The decor was of an older time, and Sam remembered this house did not belong to Zoe. She must have felt lonely; the house was huge, and she lived there all by herself. It seemed big enough to house a family of ten, and there would still be plenty of room left over.

"Zoe, are you lonely here?"

"Meeting you made my life feel fuller than it actually is."

Sam was beginning to feel guilty for being so brash on his arrival and almost forgot why he had made the trip to see her. It quickly came back to him. "Zoe, you have to stop all of this behaviour."

Zoe frowned in confusion. "*I* have to stop this behaviour?"

"Yes."

"If you didn't want to see me anymore, then you could have said so, instead of blanking me. I've tried to contact you, and you've cut me off!"

Sam was speechless. How could she sit there and blatantly lie to his face? He was also beginning to think she had gone mad. Maybe living in the house on her own after the recent death of her only remaining family member had caused it. Sam pushed his feelings of guilt to one side again and tried to remain firm. "Cut you off? I wish, Zoe. I can't breathe without you knowing about it. I tried to work my time around you and Jenny, but it wasn't working. If you can't accept Jenny being in my life, then we can't be together."

Zoe smirked. "Jenny. She has some hold on you."

"What do you mean by that?"

"She hates me because of you."

"You're deluded. Me and Jenny..." Sam couldn't finish his sentence.

Zoe had gotten up from her seat and was already shouting. "Just get out, Sam! If you can't see what's going on here, then this conversation is already over!"

Sam stood up and walked slowly over to the door, where Zoe was waiting for his exit. He shook his head, in sadness and frustration. "This could have really gone somewhere, Zoe, but you have ruined it before it even had a chance."

"I didn't ruin this, Sam," she had tears in her eyes. "Jenny, she can't stay out of our business. You need to know the things she has been saying, about you, about us."

"No!" Sam lost his temper. "You need to know you're out of order. You're right; this conversation is over." Sam proceeded to leave, but Zoe blocked his way. She grabbed his shoulders and would not allow him to move any closer to the front door.

Sam felt a rush of anger flood his veins, and he instinctively pushed Zoe, who was crying, away from him. "Get off me, Zoe. Let me out!"

"No," she sobbed. "This isn't right. I'm not crazy."

"Of course you're not. Zoe, just forget us."

Sam couldn't understand why Zoe had gotten so mad; they hadn't been together that long. And nothing had ever happened between him and Jenny for her to become so jealous. What on earth had happened to her?

He watched Zoe as she slid down the wall in a flood of uncontrollable tears, and Sam's conscience set in. He approached her slowly, bending down to her level. He saw something in her eyes, something that wasn't right. It scared him. "I'm sorry if I've hurt you. It wasn't meant to be this way."

Sam got up and tried to block out the sounds of her sobs as he closed the front door behind him. He could hear her shouting something about Jenny harassing her and saying she had been sleeping with Sam behind Zoe's back. He couldn't believe she would say such a thing just to try to keep them together. He ignored the words behind the sobs and continued to walk away. Sam wasn't a bad person, although closing the door on a crying girl made him feel pretty heartless. He really wondered why she had changed so much. Was she really feeling that threatened by Jenny? Jenny had been nothing but nice to her, and she had to go and make up lies about her. Jenny would never do anything like what Zoe had said.

Sam had to stop himself from turning back. He knew as the genuinely caring person he was known for, he should. But then, he thought of the phone calls, the threatening letters, and the general crazy behaviour, and that what he had witnessed could have all been an act. She wanted him to turn around and go back.

He decided to go for a drink, by himself, to clear his head before heading back to the flat. As much as Jenny was his best friend, and he loved her dearly, he didn't want to face her questions when he told her what had happened between him and Zoe.

***

As Sam sat at a table at the back of a small pub, a range of emotions had taken over, and he didn't know how to deal with them. He sipped on a whisky, and in his mind, he had convinced himself he had done the right thing. As much as it pained him to walk away from a woman whom he had begun to fall for, he knew for her sanity, his safety, and his friendship with Jenny it was best all round to move on.

He took his time with the whisky. He enjoyed the feeling of it warming his blood. The pub where he consumed his nerve-calmer was not the usual type of pub he would choose. It was what may be described as an old man's pub, and that was why Sam had picked it. No one would think to look for him there. He nursed the same whisky for around two hours before having the mental strength to get up and go back to the flat.

He walked home, taking in the autumnal views around him. The leaves were turning beautiful shades of red and orange, and the pavement was littered with them. They crunched as he placed his feet upon them. He heard his steps repeated behind him, although when he turned, an empty space was where he expected to see Zoe. He wondered if the house wouldn't be the last place he would see her. She wasn't going to give up without a fight. Sam wanted the end of their relationship. Could it be that simple?

***

The feet stepped over the body as it lay on the floor of the house with the old-style decor. It lay perfectly still at the bottom of the stairs on the worn carpet, and it looked unnatural. It was plain to see bones were broken.

Zoe had not known of her intruder, not at first. The intruder had followed Sam to the house, went around to the back door, and snuck inside as they had argued. The back door was in the kitchen, at the end of the hallway, and with the sitting room at the front of the house, neither Sam nor Zoe had heard the intruder enter.

As the figure crouched down over Zoe's body, a hand encased in black leather fell over the eyes to close them. The figure stood up to leave, unaware of the soul which rose too. The soul itself was disorientated and unaware of what had happened as it watched the human figure walk out of the house through the back door.

A few hours passed before reality set in. Zoe stood over her own lifeless body and wondered helplessly what would happen next.

4

Claire tried not to listen to the conversation going on at the table, but she just couldn't help herself. Knowing it was wrong, she tried to concentrate on other things, but the voices kept creeping back to her.

"So, you're going on a date with Deborah, then?" Jenny asked as she sipped at her black tea.

Claire felt Jenny's eyes on her. There was something Jenny really didn't like about her, but she had no idea what. Most likely because she was friendly towards Sam. Which was ridiculous because she was friendly to all her customers.

"Yes, I'm going to take her to the new Italian restaurant in town, then maybe on to a bar."

Jenny smiled. "It's good to see you happy and confident enough to date again."

"Please don't bring it up; it tires me out thinking about it."

"I'm not bringing up anything. God, I'm just saying it's nice to see you smile and not worry about—"

Sam cut her off. "Yes, I know. Sorry, I want to forget about Zoe and what happened. Not every girl will be like that. I want to move on and enjoy myself."

Claire had distanced herself from the table, allowing the unwanted attention from Jenny to ease off. She kept her ears on the conversation and her mind on pouring coffees.

I can't believe he's actually here, at my place of work, Claire thought, almost scalding her wrist with boiling water due to excitement. *I mean, he's actually here—it's insane.*

She listened to the exchanging words between Sam and Jenny and wondered who they were discussing. It became apparent it was an ex-girlfriend Jenny seriously didn't like. It seemed like she didn't like any female involved with Sam.

"There is no reason for you not to enjoy yourself; however, all I'm asking is that you are wary of *who* you enjoy yourself with. It was bad enough the first time, and you don't want to let your guard down and have it happen again!" Jenny sipped at the tea once more.

Sam sighed. "I know you're right. I just hate to think about it."

"Why don't you take things slowly with Deborah first off and see how it plays out? If you keep her at arm's length, then maybe you'll end up really liking her?"

"It's a trust thing, really."

"I don't blame you. I would struggle to trust someone new after what she did. Bloody psycho."

What on earth had happened? Claire thought as she listened intently, careful of her mannerism. She suddenly found herself at the table. "Is there anything else I can get for you both?"

Jenny smiled, but Claire could tell it was forced. "No, we're fine, thank you."

Sam looked up at Claire. "Thank you."

Claire nodded and returned to the counter. *He's so beautiful.*

"Okay, enough with this dreary reminiscing session. Let's get out of here and go back to the flat and open that bottle of wine in the fridge." She heard Sam say.

"I love that idea," Jenny replied.

They stood up and proceeded to approach the counter where Claire pretended not to notice his presence.

"Could we pay please?" he asked.

Claire spun round to face Sam, disappointed to see Jenny stood next to him. "Of course."

Jenny linked her arm through Sam's. She watched Jenny out from the corner of her eye as Sam held his card over the contactless payment machine to pay their bill. Jenny was stunning, with a figure to die for.

Bitch! Claire thought. Her thoughts were halted when Claire reached over to hand the receipt to Sam, and her skin connected with his. She felt her hand tingle, and her heart leapt. On connection, she raised her head and saw he had already pulled his hand away, proceeding to put his card back into his wallet.

"Was service to your satisfaction today?" Claire's voice quivered.

"Everything was fine, thank you." At his reply, she felt the heat rise from her neck, and once again, her face changed from pale to crimson in a second.

Jenny rolled her eyes.

As they left, Claire watched as she tried to control her breathing. She couldn't get her head around the fact she had served Sam Leonard. The one time she finally got to see the man whom she had followed from play to play through most of his acting career, and she was in her work attire.

Nice! I'm dressed in the worst possible apron with coffee stains on it, and this is when the universe decides to put him in my path.

Just at that, Jenny appeared back in the café, looking for something under the table where she and Sam had been sitting moments before.

"Have you lost something?" Claire called over.

"I left a bag in here," Jenny replied.

Claire walked over to the table and pulled one of the chairs out to help Jenny look.

"I can do it myself," Jenny snapped.

Claire took a step back in shock. She hadn't expected to have her head bitten off. "All right, I'm only trying to help!"

"You've done enough!"

Claire frowned at the comment. "What's that supposed to mean?"

Jenny retrieved the bag and stood up, pushing the hair away from her face. It shone beautifully in the sunlight flowing through the windows, a lovely autumn red colour.

"Just do as you're told and stay away."

"What?"

"You heard, stay away!"

Claire could see hatred in the eyes of the girl who stood in front of her. She felt as though the venom had been injected into her bloodstream, and she could feel it trickling through the veins inside her, burning as it did so.

"What the hell is your problem?" Claire stood her ground.

Jenny turned her back on Claire and made her way to the door. Before leaving, she turned to Claire and smiled. "Have a nice day," she replied sweetly, as if the last thirty seconds hadn't happened.

The bell on the door rang as Jenny walked out and left Claire, standing bewildered in the middle of the café.

"Are you okay?" a voice came from a corner table.

"Yes, thank you. Just an angry customer, I think," Claire replied to the girl who was sitting with her back to the window.

Claire felt a little shaken. *What the hell was that? Did I do something wrong?*

"I wouldn't worry about it too much. She seems the type who has to have an opinion on everything he does and everyone he sees."

Claire frowned at the girl's comment but was still distracted by what had just happened.

After a few moments, the café came to life with fashion students from the local university bustling through the doorway. Claire snapped back to reality when her ears were flooded with the sound of girly giggles and shoe chat.

She was about to turn to the counter once more before realising the girl who had been sitting in the corner was gone. She had been the only one in the café when Jenny and Sam had left. Claire hadn't seen her leave.

Come to think of it, she hadn't seen her enter, either.

5

Deborah looked in the mirror one last time before finally deciding on the dress she had tried on the first time. It had taken her almost two hours to decide on what she was going to wear. She was so nervous about finally getting a date with the man of her dreams that she wanted to look more perfect than perfection itself.

Obviously, she had already been on a date with Sam, if you could call it that. But this time was going to be the first *proper* date. *Hopefully he'll melt when he sees me in this,* she thought as she applied her lipstick.

On arrival at the Italian restaurant where Sam had arranged to meet her, she felt as though her stomach had fallen out in the taxi on the way, and her heart was going to burst. She saw him waiting in the seated area by the door, and her heart did a little dance.

"Hi." He stood to greet her. He walked over to the door where she was standing and kissed her on the cheek.

The restaurant was decorated with warm colours: oranges and reds. The walls were mirrored in places, and the floors were made up of black and red ceramic tiles. There was a bustle of chat, clinking of glasses, and the low hum of music played in the background.

"Hello," Deborah replied.

Sam walked around to her back and slid her coat off her shoulders. She almost crumpled.

"So, have you eaten here before?" Sam asked.

"No, but I'm open to new things." She smiled, her eyes twinkling.

"In that case, let's get seated, and we can sample some of this fine food."

A waiter approached them and led them to a table in the back of the restaurant where Sam had requested flowers and candles to be laid out. Deborah was impressed Sam had thought about the finer details. She had a feeling it was going to be a good night.

The waiter took their drinks order and moved away from the table. Sam motioned for Deborah to sit down before he did. *He's such a gentleman.* Deborah wanted to hide her face behind the menu to cover up her blushing. She couldn't understand why she was so nervous; she had already gone further than this, why so coy now?

"Are you okay?" Sam asked.

"Yes. A little nervous."

Sam smiled. "No need to be nervous. Relax. I don't bite."

Deborah laughed. She knew he was right, but she couldn't believe she was spending a second night with Sam Leonard, the famous Scottish theatre actor, among other things.

As the night went on, Deborah did relax and was enjoying Sam's company. He had such wonderful charm, and it was working its magic on her. The food was delicious, and the drinks were flowing, all courtesy of Sam.

"So, what do you do for a living, then, Deborah, outside of university, obviously?"

"I work in a little off-licence."

"You must see all walks of life going in and out of there every day."

"Sam," she laughed, "it's an off-licence, not Hollywood. The majority of people who come in are either still drunk from the night before or about to get drunk."

Sam laughed. "Nice."

Deborah smiled. She really had fallen for his charm, even before she had met him. She was, as far as she was concerned, his biggest fan. She didn't dare tell him that, though, in case it scared him away. She had even asked her lecturer that she do her university placement at the theatre where Sam's recent show had been running for two months. She specifically made sure she was in the same place as he was whenever she could. It scared her sometimes, how much she thought about him, how much she wanted to be around him, what she would do to make that happen.

She would never do anything to jeopardize her opportunity to meet with him again in the future, and if that meant keeping everything to herself about her need for his presence, then that was what she would do.

"Shall we get the bill and move on to a bar?" Sam asked as he poured the last of his beer down his throat.

Yes, he wants to stay out; this couldn't get any better, she thought. Deborah nodded as Sam gestured for the waiter to bring them the bill.

A few moments passed before the bill arrived. "Here is your bill, sir," said the girl who brought it to the table.

"Claire?" Sam said in a surprised tone.

The waitress looked down at him; it was Claire from the café. "Hi, Sam. How are you?"

"I'm great. What are you doing here?"

Deborah looked at them, not at all happy that another female had interrupted the attention she had been receiving from Sam.

"I work here," she said, looking around the restaurant.

"*And* the café?"

"Yes, and the café."

Deborah caught the girl's eye and gave her a warning glance.

"I'm sorry; I'm disturbing you. I'll leave you two alone."

Sam stood up. "No, you're not disturbing us."

Deborah could feel the frustration building in her as every word was exchanged between Sam and this woman.

The waitress glanced around before returning her gaze to Sam. He smiled widely. "She's not here, if that's what you are worried about."

No, but I bloody well am.

Claire smiled. "Am I that obvious? She was really pissed off the last time I was talking to you."

Sam sighed. "She's just overprotective—sorry about that. She didn't mean any harm."

"Could've fooled me!"

"Why do you say that?"

Deborah felt as though she had been forgotten about and like *she* was the one interrupting. Who the hell were they talking about, anyway, and who was this girl so rudely interrupting her date? She struggled to keep her frustration from showing.

"She came back into the café after you both left," Claire went on.

"Yes, she'd left a bag under the table."

The waitress hesitated before speaking. "She was really aggressive and told me to stay away from you!"

Sam seemed shocked by this. "What exactly happened?"

Deborah cleared her throat, allowing Sam to realise he had forgotten to introduce the girls to one another, but he smiled at Deborah and said, "Just a minute. Sorry about this."

Deborah was in shock. Where had his charm gone? And she had a sneaky suspicion this conversation would lead to the outcome she was not willing to think about. It made her sick to think he had a girlfriend, and this was what the conversation with this Claire character was all about. But then, if Sam had a girlfriend, Deborah would know about her. After all, she knew most things about him. Then again, maybe it was a point she had missed. She kept quiet.

"When she came back into the café a few minutes after you'd left, she was fishing around under the table you were sitting at. I asked if there was something I could help her with, and she went crazy, telling me to stay away from you. When I asked what the hell she was on about she turned to me and said, 'Have a nice day,' as if nothing had happened!"

Sam frowned. "Are you okay?"

"Why did she behave like that?" Claire ignored his question.

"I don't know. I think that she probably didn't mean it the way it came out."

Claire shook her head and proceeded to walk away, much to Deborah's relief, until Sam called her back.

"Claire, wait! I'm sorry that she made you feel like that. She's...protective of me."

"Is she your mother or something?"

Sam shook his head. "She's just a friend who's been there for me when I needed it most."

"Anyway, I need to get on—don't want my boss thinking I'm lazing around."

Sam took her hand and leaned in to kiss Claire on the cheek. "Sorry for the hassle."

Claire smiled. "It's okay, just make sure if you see me in the street, and she's with you, that you give me a wide berth. I can't be bothered having to deal with that again."

Sam nodded. "You have my word."

As Claire walked away from the table, Sam sat down. He looked up to see that Deborah's eyes were no longer relaxed and happy. They had an anger in them he realised was justified. "Oh my god, I'm so sorry about that. I didn't even introduce you to her."

"No, you didn't. Who was she, and more to the point, who is the other one you were talking about that bit her head off?"

"It's a long story; you really don't want to hear it."

Deborah didn't want to ask too many questions in the fear he would end up telling her to get lost. She decided on one more question, before changing the subject and forgetting the last five minutes had ever happened. "Are you involved with any of those women?"

"Not at all, I promise you. I'm a one-woman kind of guy. Claire is a waitress who served me and a friend today, and the woman who she was referring to is my best friend, who, as you may have gathered, is a little on the protective side when it comes to me." He held Deborah's hand as he explained.

Deborah accepted this, for now. But then she thought, if this woman was so protective of Sam and had a go at a stranger in a café, then what would she think of her?

Sam must have seen the look on her face. "Don't worry. Jenny will love you. She's excited to meet you."

Deborah smiled. "Okay. I'd like to meet her too. She seems very important to you."

"She's like a sister."

Sam helped Deborah on with her coat, and he led her out of the restaurant. It was cold, and the street was dazzling with car headlights. Deborah wrapped her coat around herself and hugged it close. He led her into a bar which was quiet and cosy with a real log fire burning at the back of the room. The decor was designed like a living room in someone's home. Brown leather sofas were dotted around with tables in front of them, and the walls were teal blue and mocha coloured. Above the fireplace was a large flat screen television, and the windows were dressed with thick lined mocha coloured curtains.

"Wow, it's like a house in here," Deborah said.

"That's the idea. What would you like to drink?"

"I'll have a white wine, please."

Deborah positioned herself on one of the large sofas as Sam went to the bar. She looked around and couldn't help but wonder if yet another female would appear during her date. After the lengths Deborah had gone to so she could be with Sam, it wouldn't surprise her at all.

"Hi, you're Deborah, aren't you?" A voice interrupted her thoughts.

She looked up to see a redhead standing at the end of the sofa. Deborah knew exactly who she was but wouldn't dream of allowing it to be known. "Yes, and you are?"

"Jenny, Sam's best friend." Jenny held out her hand to greet Deborah.

6

The flat was dark and empty. The windows were closed, but that didn't stop the cold air creeping in from the autumnal evening.

The bedroom doors were closed, and everything was in its original place. Sam's bedroom was in pristine condition, with a bed that looked like it had been ironed, and the window was dressed beautifully with the curtains symmetrically placed. The bottles of aftershave were also placed evenly on his dresser.

Her presence was not reflected in the mirror of the dresser, which was good. She didn't really want to look at her dead self, especially after the way she had died.

Zoe moved from Sam's room to Jenny's room, not sure how she was going to commence her plan. She couldn't get her head around what had happened to her, and she certainly was not ready to pass over to the other place. No, there was work still to do before she would be able to go anywhere. It had been over a month since she had died, and she hadn't exactly wrapped things up before passing.

Things could've gone so much better for everyone involved, but unfortunately, that was not the way things had turned out. Sam hadn't listened to anything she had had to say, and Zoe had decided it was time to give up and accept things were over between them.

How could he honestly think she would do such things to him? She had begun to fall in love with him…why would she do anything to jeopardize that?

From the day she died, it had taken her three weeks to learn how to apply a physical presence to her spirit. She had almost given up trying, but then remembered she had given up on something important to her once before and look where it had gotten her. When she had managed to catch the attention of that waitress after Jenny had given her hell, she had realized she could do something to put things right.

So, she journeyed through it, and eventually, she managed to succeed. She had finally learned how to move things using her mind, make things happen that would seem impossible to the human eye. Zoe had to make Sam see sense. She had thought from what she had said to him about Jenny as he'd walked away that he would have turned around and really listened. Of course, Zoe understood Sam would never believe Jenny was capable of such a thing, and now Zoe knew the truth, she had to make sure Sam knew before it ruined his life.

Zoe looked around, in drawers, behind the wardrobes, under the bed, but she didn't find what she was looking for. She was looking for *anything* she could use to show Sam what had really been happening and why things had gone so wrong.

She moved again, around the flat from room to room, looking to see what items she could move in order to make Sam notice things were not right. Zoe had two choices: to be subtle or frighteningly obvious. She had decided to go with subtle to start, as much as she wanted to tear the place apart, because she still cared deeply for Sam, even though she was dead. She didn't want to hurt him any more than he had been. Zoe knew she had plenty of time to get the message across; she just didn't want it to take too long.

***

"Nice to meet you," Deborah replied, all the while blazing with the urge to get up and walk out.

Jenny sat next to Deborah on the couch as Sam waited for his order at the bar. Deborah didn't want to speak, in fear of saying something catty, or worse, but she needn't have worried as Jenny did most of the talking.

"So, Deborah," Jenny said, "what are you and Sam doing tonight?"

Deborah looked through Jenny; the way she had said her name...she couldn't quite work it out. Was it sincerity in her tone, or downright sarcasm? "We actually haven't had much time to talk because people keep interrupting us!" She knew it was a slight bend in the truth, but she couldn't help herself—she was so angry.

"Oh?"

"It's okay, though, because we'll arrange another evening to really become acquainted."

Jenny flashed her bright white smile. "There's no need to worry, Debs. I'm his friend, more like his sister, in fact."

Deborah smiled. "I know that. He's told me all about you." Where the hell did she get off calling her Debs? The tension was about to reach breaking point as Sam appeared at the table.

"All good here, I hope?"

Jenny smiled. "As always. I was introducing myself."

Deborah also smiled, but inside, she was screaming. This was not what she had planned for her night at all. Hopefully, Sam would notice she wasn't happy and do something about it.

"So, it was nice meeting you, Debs, but I'm going to get off, got a long day ahead of me tomorrow at work, and I don't want to be tired," Jenny said.

"Nice to meet you too," Deborah replied, a little too chirpy.

Jenny kissed Sam on the cheek. "See you back at the flat."

Jenny left, and Deborah tried her best to hide the anger she was feeling in the pit of her stomach. There was always something getting in the way, or someone. She was so close to getting what she wanted; Sam. But yet, she still had a lot of work to do. But she was determined he was going to love her. And it didn't matter at what cost.

***

Jenny put her key in the door, and as it turned in the lock, she froze. Intuition told her something wasn't right, but she didn't know what it was. She wasn't sure if she should go any further or go back to the bar and wait with Sam.

Jenny knew she was probably being stupid. Besides, she didn't want to be the spare part at the table, and she could already tell Deborah wasn't keen on her. She wasn't sure why exactly, but she could guess it was something to do with her being Sam's best friend. They were all the same, the girlfriends, always jealous.

Her mind was back in the present time, and she decided she would investigate what had stopped her. Jenny was nervous as the tension built on opening the front door. The darkness in the hallway was deep and uninviting as she entered; she could feel it closing in on her. She felt suffocated by it and panicked as she reached for the light switch to her left. She flicked it, and as she did, the bulb made a popping sound before it flew out of the light on the ceiling and landed on the floor. Jenny screamed out at the sudden power surge, and she had to steady herself. She fished for her mobile phone in her coat pocket and fumbled with the touch screen for the light setting. She shone the light from her phone down the hallway to see if anything untoward was inside as she slowly stepped further into the flat.

She made her way down the hallway towards the kitchen where she thought she would be able to turn the light on and have it shine out. As she crept slowly, terrified to turn and face the open doors of the bedrooms in case a face met her gaze, she looked straight ahead until she reached her safe haven, the kitchen. She flipped the switch, and the light came on, much to her relief. It shone out of the kitchen and into the hall, where she instantly saw what had been making her feel uncomfortable.

As she faced her bedroom, horror was written in her expression at the message on the door of her wardrobe. She couldn't move, frozen in anticipation of what might come next. She read the message over and over, not sure what it meant or who had put it there.

Don't trust her!

The words alone were strange enough, but the medium used to display them was what freaked her out. Her red lipstick lay on the floor next to the bedroom door, and she could tell force was used to write the strange message as it was crushed out of its proper shape.

She was scared and pissed off at the same time. Who, for a start, would break into her home, and secondly, why would they write such a message with lipstick? Then, it dawned on her. Could it be Zoe? Surely she wouldn't be so desperate as to break into Sam's flat and try to scare them?

"Stupid bitch," Jenny muttered as she bent down to pick up the lipstick. When her hand connected with the tube, it felt cold, unusually cold, freezing in fact. She couldn't lift it as it stung her hand at the touch, like lifting an ice cube and holding it for too long. "Jesus!" she exclaimed, pulling her hand away.

She stood back up, and as she did, she felt a breath on the back of her neck. She twirled around to see who was there so quickly that she almost lost her balance. No one stood in the place she had expected to find her intruder. The hairs on her arms stood on end, like on a cold day when the bitter wind bites and raindrops fall onto your skin.

"Who's there?" she called out, fully aware the person wasn't going to reply with an introduction of themselves.

There was no sound, which scared her to the depths of her soul. It was too silent, until she heard the drawn-out rasp which chilled her blood.

Jenny...

She didn't know where to look, what to say. She didn't want to breathe.

Jenny...

Again, the long, drawn out rasp came and this time, Jenny decided she was leaving, regardless of who or what was in her home.

She forced her feet to leave the floor, allowing her to escape whatever it was tormenting her. She moved quickly out of her bedroom and down the hall towards the front door, without looking back. Already in her head were unpleasant images of what could be approaching her from behind, and she didn't dare look around to have her thoughts confirmed. She finally reached the door and moved out to the landing. The silence was still intense, almost like she had gone deaf.

"Now what?" she found herself saying aloud.

She moved down the stairway to the bottom of the building and to her relief, she saw Sam approaching the main door. She fell into his arms when he reached her.

"Oh my god, what is it? What happened?"

Jenny felt a wave of calm wash over her the minute that Sam spoke. "There's something in our flat," she whispered.

"What do you mean *something*?" Sam held her away and looked into her eyes.

"I mean *something*, as in I don't think it was human!"

"You mean, an animal?"

Jenny shook her head. "Something else. Something is wrong in there."

"Okay, stay calm. I'll check it out, and you wait here."

Jenny shook her head vigorously, becoming panicked again. "No, don't go in there."

"We have to go back in at some point. We live here."

Jenny knew he was right. But she didn't want him to go back in, not because of what was in there, but in case of what he might see. The message written in lipstick. If it really was Zoe who had left it, then how would Sam react? He had only just got back to normal after their breakup. She didn't want Zoe coming back into his life and attempting to ruin their friendship. However, the chilling voice was something that tampered with her rational explanation.

***

Zoe watched as Sam came quietly through the front door of the flat. She knew he was thinking Jenny was being irrational when she had said she didn't think the presence in the flat was human.

Of course, Jenny was wrong. The presence *was* human, or at least used to be. Zoe wasn't sure what to class herself as, now that she was dead.

She could feel herself aching at the sight of Sam approaching her as he walked towards her down the hallway. She still loved him with everything she had and could still feel it in her heart (even though she no longer had a physical form) when she saw him, that he was and would be the only one for her. She would wait for him for as long as it would take.

"Hello?" he called out as he threw open the doors of the rooms in the flat. "If you're in here, I strongly advise you leave within the next five seconds before you get hurt!"

Zoe knew her time was up, for the moment. She wanted to let him know she was with him, ready to protect him at any expense. She passed him and made her way to the front door, ready to leave. But before she did, she gathered her energy into her mind, and once she had enough, she lifted her hand and knocked a photo frame from the wall.

She watched him turn to face the direction of where the noise had come from. When he noticed the frame on the floor, he called out, "Jenny, was that you?"

"I'm still downstairs. Are you all right?" Her voice was strong again.

Sam moved closer to the frame which lay on the floor. He wondered to himself how it had managed to fall from its hook. It had been up there for a long time...why would it fall now?

"Yes, I'm okay. You can come up now. There's nothing in here." He cautiously picked the frame up from the floor and placed it back on the hook.

"Are you sure?"

Sam looked at the frame as it was back on the wall, and then, he turned to face the rest of his flat. He failed to mask the doubt in his voice. "Yeah, I'm sure."

Jenny appeared in the doorway at the end of the hall. "What are you doing?"

"It fell off the wall, so I'm hanging it back up," Sam replied, with little expression.

"It *fell* off the wall?"

There was silence between them for a moment, as if they were both trying to take in what had happened.

"Are you okay? You seem…weird," she asked quietly.

"What exactly happened in here? Something doesn't feel right. I feel invaded."

"Invaded?" She laughed.

Sam frowned. "It's not funny. I really don't feel right."

"I told you. I thought there was someone in here, but obviously, I was wrong."

"But you were so sure, and you were scared when I found you downstairs. What's changed?" Sam massaged his temples.

"Nothing's changed, I must have gotten it wrong," she said. "I need a coffee. You want one?"

His tone suddenly changed, and he seemed less tense. "Erm, yeah, I'll have one."

Zoe smiled as she walked out the door, knowing she had caused an unsettled feeling between them. She was glad. This was necessary.

***

Zoe had seen how distressed Sam had become after she had knocked the frame from the wall. Sam had meant, and still did mean, everything to her, so she didn't want to be the one who caused him to freak out.

Zoe watched Jenny in her bedroom, studying the picture on her phone of the little message that had been left for her. There was anger in Jenny's eyes as she read it over and over. Zoe couldn't hear her thoughts, but she knew what Jenny was thinking.

Zoe knew her work for the moment was done, so she left Jenny and Sam to have a peaceful night. But she wasn't going to be gone for long, and she would make sure everyone knew the truth. Zoe was already dead, so she had nothing else to lose.

7

Deborah took the wipe across her face, removing the make-up she had carefully applied to impress Sam. She looked deep into her own reflection in the mirror and wondered what had happened. She knew Sam had a female friend, she understood they were close and it was nothing else other than friendship, but she couldn't get it out of her head. She couldn't help but think there was something else between them. She had felt it in the air as they all sat together.

Sam had seemed oblivious to her thoughts, as did Jenny. Deborah didn't want her imagination to ring true, but she couldn't shake it off. Something had happened, or was going to happen, between Sam and Jenny. Deborah didn't know what that something was, but she knew it was going to be big, something that would change things for all them all.

She wiped her eye, leaving a smear of black mascara across her cheek. Deborah could feel the tears sting her eyes, and even though she knew she shouldn't, she couldn't help but allow them to fall.

Get a grip, she thought as she dabbed at her face with the wipe. She looked into the mirror once more and continued to remove the make-up.

The mirror resembled that of a dressing room mirror backstage at the theatre; oval with small light bulbs all around the frame, allowing the person sitting in front of it to see the whole face. Deborah loved the theatre; she loved plays and productions.

That was how she had come to know of Sam. He was the biggest Scottish theatre actor there ever was, and he had also come to appear in some small-time television dramas. Everyone knew who Sam Leonard was, especially in Glasgow.

Deborah had specifically asked her university lecturer if she could do her placement in Glasgow Royal Concert Hall. It so happened Sam's current project was showing there at the time her placement was ready to commence, at least that's what she told herself. She had impressed the concert hall staff, offering to stay on and help out when the big productions were about to start. She would show people to their seats and ensure the audience was comfortable and had everything they needed. Of course, all free of charge.

The purpose of her placement was to observe and learn how to write reviews, but the more she was in Sam's company and breathing the same air as him, she couldn't bring herself to leave, knowing he was still there. She needed to be near him, feel him around her, and most of all, she wanted to introduce herself to him. However, every time she tried to do that, something would stop her, like rehearsals or plain old nerves. What if he rejected her? What if he laughed in her face?

Deborah had decided she didn't want to face rejection and mess up her degree, so she waited. She waited until the final show, the final curtain call. She wanted to be able to meet Sam for the first time without being tied to the concert hall, and it so happened the final night of the show was her final day.

She had listened in on a conversation between cast members about a celebratory drink in a bar in town after the show had finished, and Deborah had decided to go along and try to bump into Sam.

Her plan had worked and had worked well. She didn't mention her involvement in the concert hall, or that she had become a little obsessed. She had made sure she knew everything about his work, where his schedule would take him, what his next project would be. All she had mentioned was she had seen his play that final night. He had seemed to like that she knew of him; little did he know how much.

She had scanned his home that night, as he slept beside her. She had taken in every photograph, every object. She had even gotten up to go to the bathroom and noticed there had been another room next to Sam's. The door had been slightly ajar, and Deborah could see there was a girl sleeping in there.

Deborah had found herself standing over this girl, Jenny. Deborah instantly found her irritating, even though she hadn't had a conversation with her. She didn't know anything about her, and maybe that was the problem. She knew everything there was to know about Sam, so maybe she would feel better if she knew more about Jenny. But how would she find out the things she needed to know without looking suspicious to Sam?

She decided she would start by making it look as though she knew all Sam wanted was a one-night stand. She would trick him into thinking that was all she had wanted, too.

Deborah had crept back into Sam's bedroom to retrieve her clothes, with every intention of keeping Sam's T-shirt, which she had pulled on once she had decided to have a look around.

She had dressed herself quietly and made her way to the kitchen to get her handbag. Then, she'd thought better of it. If she *left* her handbag, he'd find it and bring it to her, surely?

Deborah did one final scan of the flat, making sure she took everything in, just in case her plan didn't work and she might not find herself in the flat or his company again. As she crept past Sam's bedroom, all she wanted was to climb back into that bed and snuggle into him. But she knew this was the crucial time to leave if she wanted to find out if he really liked her. Waking up beside him in the morning wouldn't give her a true reaction. If he didn't like her, he would have to pretend, giving her a false impression. If she left at the moment she had intended, then she would know for sure.

Deborah admitted to herself it was a long shot, but if it worked, everything would be amazing. She had smiled as she continued her way down the hall with her thoughts, stopping one last time outside Jenny's bedroom. She watched Jenny sleep, wondering what would come of Sam living with another female if he got into a serious relationship. Jenny stirred, so Deborah made a quick and quiet exit.

Of course, her plan had worked as Sam had phoned her the next day and asked her out on the date.

She continued to wipe her face, all the while thinking of the disastrous date and how Jenny turning up had made her feel angry. Sam had a history with other females Deborah didn't know anything about. She began to worry as she looked at herself in the mirror.

She viewed her reflection and wondered what she was turning into. Deborah used to be strong, independent and full of drive towards a happy life with a good career. Now, all she could think about was Sam Leonard. It wasn't that she wanted him; it was that she needed him, and she knew it wasn't healthy. She wanted to stop her obsession, but it had taken her over. She could feel it in her bones and hear it in her heartbeat.

Deborah wanted Sam, and it scared her that she would stop at nothing to get him.

***

Deborah had been staring at her reflection for over an hour, unaware of the time, and that the room was bitterly cold. She snapped out of her trance and got up to close the window, only to find it was already closed.

"Where's that breeze coming from?" Deborah found herself saying out loud. She looked around her bedroom, confused by the breeze that had crept its way in without an open entrance.

Things had gone eerily quiet, and she didn't like it. She traced her movements after coming home. She had locked the door, closed the window in the kitchen, and turned all the lights out. So where was it coming from?

Just as the question came, she heard a thumping sound coming from the other side of her bedroom door. She froze in fear. "Who's there?"

There was no reply. The breeze had stopped, and so had the thumping.

"Hello?"

Deborah watched as the tiny hairs on her arm stood on end, and she felt them rise on the back of her neck too. What the hell was going on?

Deborah refused to leave her bedroom. Instead, she turned on the television and climbed into bed. She refused to let the thought of ghosts enter her mind, but she couldn't think of anything else that could have made that sound. She was too scared to leave the room to check. The fear of the unknown held her there, in her bed. She wanted to do something to take her mind off what had happened.

As she flicked through her recordings on the Sky+ box, she found the drama which starred Sam Leonard. It had been on her box for almost a year, and she listened to his voice as she drifted off, unaware of the entity still lurking in her home.

Being surrounded by the sound of his voice comforted Deborah, but she knew she needed more. She wanted Sam Leonard to belong to her and only her. She had already stopped at nothing to get what she wanted, and she was realising she didn't care who got hurt in the process, as long as it wasn't her.

8

Jenny watched Sam in disbelief. Why was he so angry? She was only doing right by him.

"Are you kidding?" Sam asked furiously. He raised his voice again. "I'm asking you a question, Jenny!"

"No, I'm not kidding. Why are you so pissed off?"

"Why am I so pissed off? I'll tell you why. The girl was serving us *lunch*, not trying to rob us. What the hell is wrong with you?"

Jenny felt a knot in the pit of her stomach.

"Well?" Sam persisted.

Jenny shook her head. "I was looking out for you. You know, after all the Zoe stuff, I thought you would appreciate it."

Sam sighed. "I do appreciate it. But that was a little different. Zoe was my girlfriend."

"Psycho girlfriend." Jenny rolled her eyes.

"She wasn't well in the head."

She could see how angry he felt about it, and it killed her to see him like this. She felt her heart wrench and instantly regretted what she had said to Claire. "Come here," she said as she wrapped her arms around him.

"I'm sorry to shout. I just don't see why you had to threaten her. She hadn't done anything wrong."

Jenny gritted her teeth but relaxed before she replied, "I know, but is being protective such a crime?" She pulled away to see his face. His eyes were sad after speaking about Zoe.

"It will be, if you keep threatening people. I'm going to meet someone eventually, Jenny, and she won't be crazy. She will be like anyone else, and you'll have to learn to trust her."

Jenny nodded. "I know," was all she could manage. She hated seeing him like this, and she certainly didn't want to be the one to make him feel this way.

"And anyway, I may have met her already."

Jenny let go of him and walked over to the kitchen sink, "Really?"

"Yep; Deborah. She really is something else."

Jenny managed a smile. "You think she's something special?"

Sam shrugged. "Who knows? But I would be happy to continue to find out. Although after last night, I'm not so sure she'll want to see me again."

"Why didn't you ask me about Claire last night at the bar, or when we got back here?"

Sam looked out of the window. "Wasn't the right time to discuss it."

"Are we okay?" Jenny asked apprehensively.

Sam smiled. "I can't stay angry at you. But tone it down, Jenny. Not every girl I see or even talk to is going to turn out crazy."

Jenny smiled again, knowing he was right but not willing to admit it. "So, Deborah wasn't too keen on me appearing last night, was she?"

"Considering Claire had turned up at our table discussing your antics, I'm not surprised. But don't worry, once you meet her properly, you'll be able to show her how nice you really are." Sam flashed his charming grin. "Listen, I have to get going to see what the reviews are saying about the final night of the play. I'll see you later. If anything weird happens in here again, let me know straight away, okay?"

Jenny nodded. She worried Zoe wouldn't stop her harassments. The lipstick message was easy to hide from Sam, and yes, since he had ended things, the letters and the phone calls had ceased. But what if the lipstick message was the beginning of it all again? Girls didn't treat Sam like a normal guy. They were all giggly and stupid around him, and Zoe had been so besotted she had tried to drive a wedge between him and Jenny. What if she kept coming back? Jenny pondered with the idea that she should tell Sam about the message, but decided against it. He had found Deborah and seemed happier than he had been in a while. Jenny didn't want to be the one to spoil that.

9

There was a strong stench of death and decay as DS Paul Preston entered the manor house he and DC Jim Lang had been called to earlier. It lingered in the air, and soon would linger in their nostrils and cling to their clothing. The forensics had been there for an hour or so before their arrival, and the area around the house had been taped off by the uniformed officers, who were standing guard at the bottom of the drive.

"Oh dear, this doesn't look good," Lang said as he examined the entrance hall. He looked at the body on the floor at the bottom of the stairs and grimaced at the angle of the left leg. "I think this leg is broken."

"You think?" Preston replied. Being used to Lang's sarcasm, he brushed it off.

The forensic team busied themselves around the two men as they continued to look around the house. It was an impressive property; a manor house in its day, one of the many large houses in the Glasgow area. Over the years, its decor had tired and was in good need of some renovation work, but its current state was liveable. There were picture frames all over the walls, and each one was a family picture, with many different faces. The body that lay on the floor looked to be the youngest in the photographs.

The forensic team were dusting surfaces for fingerprints as Preston retrieved a pair of gloves from one of the younger members of the forensic team. Preston had worked in the force for years, but it never got any easier seeing a dead body, especially if it had been a possible murder. The face was unrecognisable due to the length of time the body had been there, and the colour of the corpse suggested time of death had been around four weeks previous to their arrival.

Preston was no coroner, but after years of experience, he was becoming more aware of time scales in death. It still sickened him a little, but the smell was the worst thing about it. He sometimes struggled to remind himself a corpse that had lain for this long had once been a person; it was hard to imagine, what with the colour and change in appearance. His thoughts were interrupted by his colleague's voice.

"Do you think she was pushed?"

Preston shrugged. "I'm not sure. It's a fifty-fifty chance at the moment, since we've only just found her. What did the informant say, exactly?" He gestured for them to leave and allow the forensics team to get on with their jobs.

Lang sighed. "Not much, to be honest. Apparently, a local florist, who delivers flowers here on a monthly basis, hadn't received payment and had tried to phone to see if everything was all right. When she couldn't get through, she decided to drop by to check in person. She knocked on the door a few times, and when no one answered, she looked through the letterbox and saw the deceased lying on the floor."

"Do we have a name for the deceased?" Preston asked, crossing the threshold and savouring the fresh air that filled his lungs.

"Yep," Lang checked his notebook from his breast pocket. "Zoe Henderson."

Preston pulled his gloves off. He looked back into the house and at the girl, now known as Zoe, and shook his head. "Okay, we need to speak to this florist, see if she noticed anything unusual about the house when she came to check on her, anything which may have been out of place."

"She's waiting in the car with uniform. We can chat to her in a minute," Lang said.

"Yes, we need to check Zoe's phone records, see who she's been in contact with. Maybe there's a boyfriend or someone we can talk to who might've been close to her."

"Aye, you get on that back at the station. Let's question the florist, and let's see what we can come up with. You never know. It could've been a genuine accident."

"Here's hoping. A house this size, someone could've been after her money."

Lang nodded. "The world's not short of a greedy bugger, right enough."

The officers headed towards the marked police car, where the florist who had discovered Zoe was waiting. Preston opened the door to find the woman distraught, barely able to catch a breath.

"She's been like this for the last hour. I can't get her to calm down," the uniformed officer said.

Preston and Lang looked at each other and then back to the woman.

"Can we ask you a few questions?" Preston asked gently.

The woman looked up and nodded, her tear-filled eyes spilling over as she got out of the car.

"Thank you. We just need to confirm with you what happened," Lang said.

There was a pause, the woman looked across at the house and back to the officers before vomiting at their feet.

"I don't think we're going to get much sense out of her right now. Maybe we can interview her when she is in a fitter state?" Lang said to Preston.

Preston nodded as the uniformed officer consoled the woman. They retrieved contact information before leaving the woman to continue throwing up. The forensic team were busying themselves around the house and grounds, searching the property for any kind of clue which would explain Zoe's death.

"If anything crops up, no matter how small, contact either myself or Lang at the station right away. Got it?" Preston called out. The team stopped, and there were muffled replies of agreement before they continued with the search.

The officers made their way around the property, taking in the surrounding grounds and the rest of the house. Reaching the back garden, which was also extensive, Preston and Lang stopped as they came across a burial plot.

"Bloody hell," Lang said as he stared down at the stones.

"Why would you have people buried in your back garden?" Preston asked.

"To keep everyone together?" Lang said. He turned to face the manor. "This place is creepy."

The gravel crunched under the officers' shoes as they made their way back to the car. The driveway was extensively large, and they had parked at the entrance. The weather matched their mood, with grey clouds hanging over Glasgow's West End. Clouds always seemed to hang over the city, especially if there was a death to deal with. Preston had seen enough dead bodies in his time, and so some would suggest he would be used to it by now, but it never did get easier. Perhaps it was the father in him, knowing someone's child was the victim always got to him. His family meant everything, and he was never fully relaxed knowing there were crazy people out there, willing to kill—sometimes for no other reason than because they could. He had come to accept the fact since the day he had welcomed his first daughter into the world, he never would feel relaxed again. He was definitely a soft touch when it came to his girls, but if anyone ever tried to mess with them, God help them.

When Ross Turner had been on the rampage, Preston's heart had been in his throat the whole time. Ross had targeted young women, like his beautiful girls, and Preston had been quietly terrified they would fall prey to his sadistic way of thinking. Thankfully, they hadn't, and Preston was grateful for that, but still sorry someone else had to deal with their daughter's murder. He remembered Mrs Noble, the mother of Angela Noble, and the state she'd been in when they had gone to see her with the psychic, Patrick. Preston had remained professional, but remembered thinking he never wanted to feel her pain.

He thought back to when he and Lang had worked with Patrick during that case and wondered what would have happened had Patrick not had the link to Ross Turner. As much as it pained him to think it, they may never have identified the killer.

"You all right there, Paul?" Lang asked.

"Aye, let's head back to the station and get stuck into this. The sooner we know what happened to the girl, the better."

They reached the car and climbed in. Lang brought the engine to life and slowly eased out of the driveway. "Some size of house, isn't it? I mean, why was a girl like her living here by herself?"

Preston shook his head. "Maybe been left to her in a will. We'll find out more about her when we speak to the florist, who, by the way, seems to be the only person to have brought attention to this death."

"Aye, that's a bit strange. Suppose we'll have to see what her phone records say. We'll be able to get a feel for who she was in contact with, see if any of her friends know if anything has happened which could have led up to her death. How long do you think she had been lying there?"

"I'd say around four weeks, Jim. The stench was unbelievable, and her face was pretty much gone. But we'll wait for the coroner to get an accurate time of death. You never know: she may not have died immediately, or she could have been alive and then died later. Either way, I'm not sure."

"Poor kid. What a waste," Lang said, pulling up to a set of traffic lights.

Preston looked up, realising they were on South Street and wondering how Patrick was getting on since deciding not to work with them after the Turner case. "What do you think Mr McLaughlin has been doing since we last saw him?"

"Ghost hunting, most likely," Lang said; his sarcastic attitude was never far away when the subject of psychics was brought to the table.

"Ghost hunting?" Preston raised one eyebrow and smiled.

"I don't know, conjuring up spirits, or whatever it is he does."

"Still not convinced, then?" Preston laughed.

"Never will be, no matter what happens in front of me. That Turner case was all coincidental, as far as I'm concerned. The guy turned out to be his bloody brother, for god's sake."

Preston knew Lang would never accept Patrick fully, and it was fair enough. "If you say so, Jim."

"I do say so, Paul. I did come to like Patrick in the end, but no one on this earth could change my mind about death and the afterlife. In my opinion, when you're dead, you're dead, and that's the end of it. I don't know, maybe he's good at guessing."

They both laughed. Lang may not have ever said it out loud, but Preston knew even if psychics were proven to be one hundred percent legit, Lang would never back down. He had been secretly glad Patrick had turned down the offer; he didn't want to be known to anyone as the officer who relied on the word of a psychic. Patrick had told Lang particular things he couldn't have known about when they were investigating the Turner case, and at first, Lang had begun to loosen up about the whole psychic thing, but not long after that, he was back to his old sceptical self.

The discussion came to a close when they pulled up to the station in Pitt Street. The weather had gone from dull and grey, to rain pelting down from the heavens, and as Preston and Lang got out of the car, they ran to the entrance, trying to save their suits from looking like they'd just been in the washing machine.

"Come on, Jim. We've a lot to get through."

As they made their way down the corridor, Lang stopped at the coffee machine. "Fuel for the mountains of paperwork we're bound to have to go through?"

"Aye, better make it a strong one. I'll get in contact with the florist; hopefully, her stomach has settled. Clearly never seen a dead body before," Preston replied.

"Who'd want to, especially the state that poor girl was in. No wonder she was sick," Lang said.

10

Lang had trailed through endless amounts of Zoe Henderson's phone records, looking for anything he could use to find out what had actually happened to her. He had written down a few numbers and found out who the servers were, allowing him to match names to the phone numbers. There were a lot of call records, made and received, and they spanned over a number of weeks leading up to Zoe's death. He sat back on his chair, running his hand over his head, and then pinching the bridge of his nose. He wasn't so sure how he was going to explain to Preston that he recognised two of the names on the records. Of course, Glasgow was a big city, and there were likely to be several hundred people with the same name, so surely this had to be coincidental. He watched as Preston entered the office, coffee in one hand and a stack of papers in the other.

"How are you getting on with those phone records, Jim?"

Lang sighed. "There are a handful of numbers on here spanning over a few weeks; it seems like Zoe Henderson had hardly any contacts."

"Okay, so where are we headed to first?" Preston blew into the plastic cup, allowing the steam to float up around his face.

"Paul, you'd better come and sit down. There's something I need to ask you about these records."

Preston frowned. "What's wrong?" He sat down on the seat next to Lang.

"I've been going through these records, and the same numbers have been cropping up from calls made and received, apart from the odd call centre number. So, I got in touch with the providers and got the names of the accounts linked to the numbers." He stopped, not sure where to take it next.

Preston gestured, moving his hand in circular motions telling Lang to continue. "And?"

Lang slid the records across to Preston, allowing him to look for himself. Preston lifted the paper, and his eyes scanned over it. Lang watched as he read each name, and as he expected, Preston's eyes stopped over the two names he knew would catch his attention.

He looked up at Lang and simply said, "Shit!"

Lang nodded. "Do you recognise the number next to the names?"

Preston pulled his phone out of his pocket and scanned through the names in his contacts list. "I don't memorize numbers, Jim. That's what these things are for. I need to check the numbers."

A few moments passed where Preston stared at the phone then the paper. "Aye, they match."

Lang sighed heavily. "It's nothing to worry about, Paul. We'll sort it."

"Sort it? My daughters' names are on Zoe Henderson's phone records. Whether it was murder or not, I have to go and tell them a friend of theirs has been found dead."

"Do you know she was a friend of theirs?" Lang asked, trying not to sound too accusing.

"She's not family, so I can't see any other way they would know her."

Lang nodded again. He knew Preston's daughters' involvement with Zoe would be innocent, but he had to go down every avenue of scrutiny until they were sure Zoe's death was accidental. "We'll both go to see them, but I think I should do the talking. You're the father, after all; you have to have some separation."

"Aye, I know. Let's go and get this over with."

***

The journey to the Preston household was quiet. Preston never liked to allow work and home life to come together, but with this, he didn't see he had much choice. The weather had turned nasty, and the rain battered off the windscreen as the wipers fought to keep it clear. With the rain came the dip in temperature, and this followed the dip in Preston's mood. "Why did I pick this as my career?"

"Because, you love to catch the baddies, Paul. You've always been good at it," Lang replied, keeping his eyes on the road.

As they pulled up to the house, the rain didn't do them any favours, and in fact, it seemed to get heavier. Preston and Lang got out of the car and ran the ten yards to the front door. Preston turned to Lang who was behind him. "Wipe your feet; my Janet will go mental if you get mud on the floor."

"That's what you're worried about now?" Lang shook his head.

Janet Preston came out from the large kitchen at the back of the house with an apron around her and oven gloves on. "What are you both doing here? Hi, Jim. Would you like a drink?"

Lang nodded. "Tea would be great, Jan, thanks."

"I have to speak to the girls. Are they home?" Preston asked.

"What's wrong, Paul?" She sounded nervous.

Janet Preston was a proper housewife and stay-at-home mum, even though their two daughters were in their twenties and at university. Her physical health had deteriorated in the last few years. Having slipped a disc in her neck when making the bed one Saturday morning, Paul insisted she give up her job in hairdressing. She had loved it dearly, but with it being such a demanding job and causing her to be on her feet all of the time, she agreed.

Janet still coloured and styled Lisa and Jane's hair and cut Preston's when the sides became wispy, but that was about as far as it went. She did miss her job, the social side and the constant development of hair styling, but she would never go back to it. Her body wouldn't allow it as she struggled to do the weekly food shop and couldn't carry more than two full bags without her neck becoming unbearably painful. Now, she lived for her family, cooking meals for her and Paul every night, making sure the girls were well equipped for their university course, and her weekly book club. Janet was happy with her life and wouldn't change it now.

"Something has happened to someone the girls know, and we need to ask them a few questions," Lang answered for him.

"I'll go upstairs and bring them down. They're studying."

Janet could just be heard climbing the stairs, her feet barely making a sound on the wooden slats that lined the floor. She was a petite woman, with a small frame and very slim face. Her light brown hair was shoulder length, and her eyes were a clear blue. Preston often thought of the ocean on the sunniest of days when he looked into her eyes—it was one of the many reasons as to why he fell in love with her.

"Are you going to be okay with this, Paul?" Lang asked.

"They're my girls, Jim; it's better if this comes from me. So long as there is nothing sinister in it, which I whole-heartedly believe there isn't…"

They heard footsteps above them, approaching the top of the stairs, and the muffled voices of Lisa and Jane Preston as they descended them, unaware of the knot in their dad's stomach. Lisa Preston was a twenty-six-year-old student teacher at Glasgow University and on her second year, and Jane Preston was twenty-four and a drama and dance student at the Royal Scottish Academy of Music and Drama. Both girls led very different lives and were quite close. They shared the same group of friends and went out together as often as their busy schedules would allow them to. The girls adored their dad and were often referred to as 'daddy's girls' by their mum.

They entered the living area with beaming smiles and hugged their dad as if they hadn't seen him in a week.

"Hi, Dad. What's up?" Jane asked.

"Hi, Jim," Lisa added as Janet hurried by them to the kitchen.

"Girls, have a seat. I have a few things that I want to ask you." Preston sat down on the single recliner in front of the window. The rain had stopped.

The girls sat down on the sofa next to the door. "What is it, Dad?" Lisa asked.

Preston took a breath. "Are you both friends with a girl named Zoe Henderson?"

Both girls gave their full attention on hearing Zoe's name. "Yes, she's our friend," said Lisa. "She's in my course at uni, although she has been on placement, so I haven't seen her for a few weeks."

"She's lovely, but I think she's a bit lonely. She has this *massive* house that was left to her in a family will. Don't think she wants it, to be honest, but I can't see why—it would be an amazing party house," Jane added.

"What's happened to her?" Lisa asked. "You wouldn't sit us down and ask about a random friend if everything was okay."

Preston could see Lisa was worried; Jane, on the other hand, was a little slow at picking up on where the conversation was headed. "Something has happened to her; we're not sure what yet. But she was found dead this morning."

Jane's expression changed then, from pure oblivion to utter devastation. "Dead? Are you sure, Dad?"

Lisa's eyes had filled with tears, and her bottom lip quivered. "What do you mean she was *found* dead? Where?"

"At the bottom of the staircase in her house," Lang cut in before Preston. "We're not sure if she fell or..."

"Was pushed?" Lisa suggested.

"We're going to be looking at all lines of enquiry. But we need your help. We need to know more about Zoe, who she was friends with, where she went out, who she was seeing—that sort of thing."

Janet appeared with box of tissues and sat down by the girls. Preston loved the maternal instinct she possessed. "Okay, Paul. Tell the girls what you need to know."

Preston felt a mixture of emotions as he watched his wife take control of the situation. She was the family rock who everyone leaned on when times were tough, and for such a little woman, she sure as hell knew how to put a brave face on a tough situation.

"Yes, so, like Jim said, we're not one hundred percent sure yet if Zoe's death was accidental, and we need more information about her and her life which will help us to determine that."

"How did you know she's our friend?" Lisa asked.

"We tracked down her phone records. There were only a handful of numbers on it, and yours were in amongst them," Lang answered.

Lisa nodded. "Okay. So, what can we do to help?"

"We would like a list of names: friends, boyfriends, that sort of thing." Lang had taken control of the discussion; he could remain impartial, and at some point in the investigation, Paul would be able to distance himself from Lisa and Jane's involvement once they had done their bit.

"Let me get my phone and a notepad and pen, and I will write everything down that I know." Lisa got up and went upstairs to her bedroom, and Jane followed her.

"Can you believe this?" Lisa asked as she rummaged in her bedside table for her notepad. She could feel the tears sting the corners of her eyes but fought against them.

"That our friend may have been murdered? No, I can't believe it!" Jane's hands trembled as she took her phone off the charger dock. "How can you be so calm?"

Lisa took a deep breath. "It's not without difficulty. Come on, Zoe was our friend, and she would want us to help her. Let's get this over with."

Lisa held Jane's hand, and together, they faced their friend's death.

11

It didn't take long for the girls to give Preston and Lang the information they needed to take their enquiries further. It seemed Zoe Henderson hadn't had that many friends, and she had been the last remaining member of her family—according to Lisa.

"Why was she living in that huge house by herself?" Preston had asked.

Even though Lisa was struggling to keep her emotions at a level of control, she was determined to answer as many questions as she could to help her friend. "She was the last remaining Henderson; she said the house had been in her family for over a century, and that it would remain that way until they died out, if they ever did. She was a private girl, but I do remember her saying she wanted to have children of her own so she could carry on the bloodline—she wanted to keep her own name so the house would always be 'Henderson Manor.' It's so sad that will never happen now."

Lang was scribbling everything down on his notepad, and Preston was nodding along as Lisa spoke. "She thought she would marry Sam, but it wasn't going too well."

"What do you mean?" Lang stopped writing.

"They kept arguing, apparently." Jane wiped a tear from her cheek.

"What would they argue about?" Preston went on to ask.

"Zoe was pretty private. She mentioned they argued about stuff to do with his best friend, but she never really elaborated on it." Lisa lowered her head as she spoke.

Lang looked out of the window. The sun had broken through the clouds, and the wet ground glistened in the brightness. "Could you give me more information on this Sam character, please?"

Jane looked to Lisa. "I can't do this, Lisa," Jane said. "I feel sick talking about her in the past tense. I feel sick at the thought that she's dead."

Lisa took her hand; she was always the stronger of the two, and she was always intent on looking after her little sister no matter what the situation. "His name is Sam Leonard. They were together for a while. She seemed really happy when they first started seeing each other, but then, she started acting really strange."

"In what way?" Lang pushed.

"I don't know...she was a little distant and was always blaming their arguments on his friend."

"And what's this friend's name?"

"I don't know. Like I said, she never gave too much away when it came to her relationship."

"Do you think she was killed on purpose, Dad?" Jane asked.

Preston smiled. "We don't know anything yet, sweetheart, but we'll find out what happened to her. I promise."

Lang turned from the window to face Lisa. "Hang on...Sam Leonard you say?"

"Yes."

"Sam Leonard, the actor guy?" Lang asked.

Lisa nodded. "So she said. At first, I didn't believe her, but then, she showed me a picture of the two of them, and I had no choice but to believe her."

"You were never in their company when they were together?" Preston asked.

"No, again, like I said, she was very private and didn't like to broadcast her relationship, maybe because he's so well known."

Preston and Lang stood up and smiled at the girls. "Thanks girls, you've been more than helpful," Lang said.

"I'll see you tonight, girls. I'll try to be home for dinner." Preston said.

Janet's voice came from the kitchen door. "I'll keep some food by for you, if you aren't home on time, Paul."

The girls made their way back upstairs, and Preston kissed his wife goodbye before he and Lang left the house. They got into the car, and Preston pinched the top of his nose. "I can't believe this."

"They're nothing but innocent in all of this, Paul, so don't you worry about them. They're strong girls, and they'll deal with this." Lang placed his hand on Preston's shoulder.

"I know, Jim, but I hate that they're involved at all."

Lang started the engine. "We need to have a chat with the florist. Maybe she'll know something to link with what the girls have said."

"Aye, maybe, but I'm not so sure anyone other than Sam Leonard will be able to help us."

Lang drove out of Preston's street and along to the main road. The rain was falling again and along with it, hailstones.

Preston took the note from the dashboard that contained the florist's shop address and read it aloud. "Lynne's Flowers, Hyndland Road."

Lang nodded. "That's not far from here, five minutes. In fact, that isn't far from Henderson Manor."

"It would make sense she used a florist nearby."

"Hopefully, she's feeling a little less fragile than she did," Preston said.

"Well, even if she's not, we need to speak to her today, otherwise her information will go stale."

"We should go easy, though. We don't want to put the pressure on. She discovered a dead body going about her daily business; she's bound to be distressed. You remember what you were like when you saw your first."

"My stomach still flips now. It's the smell, Paul. I can't stand the smell. And the longer they've been dead, the slimier the body seems to get. Like a bag of mush."

Preston shook his head. "Thanks for that, Jim."

***

Before they knew it, they had arrived at the little purple and yellow shop which was sandwiched in between a café and an independent bookshop. They parked outside and went in to see the owner, fully expecting a woman in pieces.

When they were inside, the gentle scent of various flowers filled their nostrils. A little bell above the door rang out pleasantly, to make the staff aware of the potential customer. The shop floor was colourful with flowers, which Preston and Lang had no clue of their names—the only flowers Lang could name were roses and daffodils, and Preston was much the same.

"I'll be with you in a second," a female voice came from a room at the back.

"It's DC Lang and DS Preston, Ms Prowse. We're here about Zoe Henderson," Lang called back.

Lynne Prowse popped her head out of what Lang had decided was the stock room. "Oh, of course. I'll shut the shop while we chat. Tea?"

Lang looked back at the seemingly chirpy woman, assuming she felt the need to pretend she was fine. Of course, Lang knew she was not. Her expression didn't match her tone. The horrified look on her face didn't go well with the happiness in her tone.

"No thanks, Ms Prowse. We'll make this as quick as possible," Preston replied.

Lynne Prowse came out from the stock room and stood behind the serving desk, placing her hands on the counter. "I'll try to be as helpful as I can. I just can't believe she's dead. Zoe was such a loyal customer."

"Are you all right, Ms Prowse?" Lang asked.

The woman hesitated for a moment, the smile on her face finally falling as tears filled her already reddened eyes.

"We understand what you saw can have a profound effect. You don't have to pretend with us," Preston said.

It was then that the tears fell, uncontrollable sobs left her chest, her shoulders shaking as she tried to control herself. "I'm sorry. I just can't get it out of my head. It looked..." She trailed off.

"Yes, it's not pleasant. But remember, whatever happened to Zoe, she isn't suffering now. Hopefully, you can take some peace from that," Lang said. He glanced at Preston and motioned to his notepad. Now would be a good time to start asking questions, giving Ms Prowse something to focus on other than the dead body.

"How often did you deliver flowers to Zoe?" Preston asked, opening the first page.

"Zoe gave me instructions to deliver white lilies and purple pansies at the beginning of every month. She would always pay directly into my business account on the last day of the month—in advance, you'll understand."

"And why is it she had flowers delivered every month?" Lang asked.

Lynne shrugged. "She liked to put fresh flowers on the family burial plot to keep it looking nice, you see."

"Yes, we noticed that," Preston said.

"They date back a century, I think."

"Okay, Ms Prowse, did you notice anything about Zoe the last time you saw her?"

Lynne shook her head. "No. Like I said, I delivered lilies and pansies to her at the beginning of every month, and the only words that were ever exchanged were pleasantries. I knew nothing about the girl."

Preston believed her. "Okay, Ms Prowse. Thank you for your time, and if you have any more information or think of anything else, then please do contact us." He handed his card over.

"Good day to you, Ms Prowse," Lang said as they left.

On leaving the shop, Lang thought about Lynne's statement and was unsure if there would be anything from it that would help their enquiry. "On to Sam Leonard's house, then?"

"Aye, back to the station first, though. I want a bit of background information on him before we begin questioning. He's the only one whose number is on her records and had the most contact with over a certain number of months, so I want to make sure we have all the relevant information on him that we need before we question him."

They climbed back into the car, and Preston drove them down Hyndland Road and crossed over Byres Road. The little cafés and delis were empty on account of the rain, and the roads were jammed with cars and buses. No one wanted to be out in the crazy weather Preston and Lang had experienced over the course of the day. They drove down University Avenue, and the huge trees sheltered the street from the pelting rain, which had, once again, begun to fall.

"So, any thoughts on this?" Lang asked as they proceeded to cross the lower end of Sauchiehall Street and then turned left onto Argle Street.

"Aye, I think Sam Leonard will be able to help us out with this. Even if the relationship had gone sour, and the girl was so devastated, she had killed herself, it would still put an end to the enquiry."

Lang nodded. "Maybe you're right."

Preston pulled up outside the station and killed the engine. "Okay, let's see what we can find on this Sam Leonard."

The sun made another break in the clouds and shone down as they walked into the station.

12

S am Leonard stood in front of the mirror as he brushed his teeth and watched the paste foam up and spill over his lips. He thought about what to do with his day off and wondered if he should contact his agent to see if any of the theatre productions coming up had shown an interest in him since his last performance. The bathroom smelled like men's shower gel, and the condensation from the hot water in the shower ran down the gleaming white tiles. Sam felt good and was happy, finally feeling like his personal life was getting back to normal.

Deep in his daydream, he heard Jenny call out for him from the end of the hall. He wrapped a towel around himself and popped his head out of the ensuite shower room. "What's up?"

"There are some people here who want to talk to you," Jenny replied, her voice uneasy.

Sam frowned. "Who is it?"

"It's the police."

Without warning, Sam's stomach flipped making him feel instantly nauseous. What would the police want? He quickly dried himself off and threw on a pair of stonewashed denims and a black T-shirt. He reached for the handle on the bedroom door and made his way into the hall, where he observed two men, each dressed in a suit. One was taller than the other and slimmer, the short one was plump, a size Sam did not care to think about for when he reached middle age himself. Putting on his most confident gleaming smile, he said, "What can I do for you, gentlemen?"

"I'm DS Preston, and this is DC Lang." Preston paused as Sam nodded.

"We would like to talk to you about a Miss Zoe Henderson," Lang replied.

"Can we sit down?" Preston asked.

Sam felt another lurch in his stomach. "Yes, let's go through to the sitting room."

Jenny followed Sam, and the two officers into the sitting room and sat down beside Sam. "Can you confirm you know Zoe Henderson?" Preston asked.

"Yes, she's my ex-girlfriend." Sam swallowed hard. He was quite sure he knew what was coming next from the officer, but he didn't want to hear it.

"We were called out to a property in Winton Drive earlier this morning, where Zoe Henderson was found dead."

Sam's stomach contents were like a demon trying to break free from hell. He made it to the bathroom just in time, spilling his guts like someone who had eaten a dead animal. The violent wretches caused pain to his sides and temples, but he managed to control his breathing and compose himself before returning to the sitting room.

"Are you okay?" asked Jenny, who'd gone pale.

"Yeah, sorry about that." Sam felt ashamed with his reaction; he really had thought Zoe couldn't affect him anymore. He guessed he was wrong.

"Mr Leonard, we would like to ask you some questions about your involvement with Zoe Henderson," Preston said.

Sam placed his hand over his abdomen again, willing his stomach to control itself. "Of course."

Lang retrieved his trusty notebook from the breast pocket of his jacket and flipped it open. He allowed Preston to do most of the questioning, giving him time to write everything down.

"So, Mr Leonard, can you confirm the last time you saw Zoe Henderson?"

Sam cast his mind back to the day he'd ended their relationship; they hadn't parted on particularly good terms. "Around a month ago, maybe more. I'm not sure." Sam watched as DC Lang scribbled in his pad.

"Maybe more?" Preston asked.

"I don't keep a list of dates and times, if that's what you mean," Sam replied, annoyed by Preston's tone.

"Okay, and could you tell us about the conversation that took place on that day?"

Sam hadn't allowed himself to think about Zoe at all since their break-up, let alone think about the day he left the only woman who he'd ever had feelings for. "We broke up the last time I saw her." The sentence hung in the air, hovering over everyone in the room. Sam understood Preston wasn't going to allow it to hang over them for any length of time, so he carried on. "She had become a little, shall we say, obsessed. I couldn't cope with it, so I ended it."

The room would have been silent, if it weren't for the scraping of Lang's pen. He looked up from the notebook. "Obsessed with what?"

"Me. She was obsessed with me."

Lang glanced at Preston before continuing. "Please elaborate, Mr Leonard."

"She was stalking me."

Preston's brow furrowed. "Your own girlfriend was stalking you?"

"She was always a little jealous my best friend happens to be female, and so, from the offset, she and Jenny never really got on."

"Jenny?"

"That's me. Jenny Lawson," Jenny replied.

"So, you never got along with Zoe. Why was that?" Preston asked.

Jenny shook her head. "Sam told you why: she didn't like that Sam and I are best friends. She couldn't accept he had another female in his life, and that we lived together. She was always nice to my face, and I never had any qualms she would come between Sam and I, so I tried to be nice and let her see I wasn't a threat."

Sam was grateful Jenny was aiding the interview, if, in fact, that's what it was, an interview. He couldn't get his head around the fact Zoe was dead. She was *actually* dead, and the police were questioning, he guessed, his involvement.

"It didn't bother you that your best friend's partner had a problem with you?" Lang asked.

"I didn't say it didn't bother me. I said I tried to be nice and prove I wasn't a threat."

"So, what happened when you *were* nice to her?"

Jenny took a deep breath. "*Nothing* happened. When I was nice or pleasant or kind or anything else that may be interpreted as friendly, she would either ignore me or put on a sarcastic smile. She was always careful not to do it in front of Sam."

"And why was that?" Preston replied.

Sam interrupted. "She would've known I wouldn't stand for it. Jenny has been in my life since we were little, and I'm not the sort to let a relationship with a woman tear apart my friendships."

All four fell silent for a few moments and the only sound to be heard was, once again, the scribble of Lang's pen.

Sam hung his head low, his chin almost touching the top of his chest. "Are we done here?"

Preston nodded. "I'd say we're almost done here. I know this must be very difficult for you, but if you could just answer a few more questions, we'll be able to eliminate you from our enquiries."

Sam lifted his head. "You're saying I'm a suspect in Zoe's death?"

Jenny got to her feet. "That's bloody ridiculous."

"I'm saying this is procedure, and we're trying to establish Zoe's last few hours before she died. We're not saying whether her death was intentional or not," Preston replied, as if reassuring them.

"Okay, but please make it quick," Sam said, accepting Preston's words.

"So, Sam, can you tell us what your relationship was like with Zoe before you split?" Lang interjected.

Sam cast his mind back and remembered how much he had adored her, and how she was always smiling and laughing, but then, things changed quickly. She was always quiet around Jenny and never made an effort to speak to her or at least be civil. "Things were fine in the beginning, like a normal relationship. We were always going out for dinner, drinks, that sort of thing. Then, I introduced her to Jenny, and Zoe went weird."

"Weird, in what way?" Lang pressed.

"She would never want to speak *to* Jenny or *about* her. She was jealous, and I confronted her about it. Of course, she denied it, but she never did anything to change the way she was around her."

"I tried to make things better between us," Jenny added. "But she just wasn't interested. I didn't want Sam to feel awkward when Zoe was in the flat and I was there. In the end, I realised it wasn't me who had to change. She was an oddball, if you ask me."

"Jenny and I were getting anonymous text messages, phone calls and letters, among other things."

"From whom?" Preston asked.

"We couldn't prove it, but we were pretty certain it was Zoe. We were getting typed letters through the door, saying things like, 'I hate you, Jenny Lawson,' and 'You're a home wrecker,'" Sam said.

"Sounds like someone was jealous, but does that necessarily mean it was Zoe?" Lang commented.

"That's what I thought, at first, but there was no one else I could think of."

"There were also photographs with the letters, of Sam and I together having coffee, or at the pub," Jenny added. "It was freaking me out, so Sam said he was going to end things with her. I said that doing so would make things worse, but he went ahead and did it anyway."

"So, how did Zoe react when you ended the relationship?"

"As you can imagine, she didn't take it too well. She was incredibly upset and swore blind she hadn't sent any of the hate mail to us. Then, as I was leaving, she shouted something about Jenny being the one who was sending the letters and making the phone calls, which is ridiculous. To be honest, by that point, I didn't care if it was Zoe or not; our relationship was doomed from the *first* moment she shared her dislike and jealousy for Jenny. It had to end, regardless of the hate mail. What made the whole situation worse was I had fallen for her. Apart from all the crazy behaviour, she was actually a good laugh. We got on so well, and I was genuinely sad when I decided the best thing to do was to end it."

Both officers nodded as they listened. "I think we have everything we need here. Thank you for your co-operation. We'll be in touch if we have any developments," Preston said as he stood up. Sam and Jenny joined him.

Lang put his notepad back into his breast pocket and stood up. He shook Sam and Jenny's hands and followed his colleague to the front door.

Sam closed the door, and Jenny hugged him tight. "Are you okay?" she asked.

"I think I'm in shock. She was fine when I left her, well, not *fine*, but you know what I mean."

"Sam, I don't think Zoe would have killed herself because you ended things with her. She didn't seem like that sort of person, despite everything else."

"I'm not sure of anything. I mean, we will never *really* know if she was the one sending all of those photos and messages and making the silent phone calls, but everything that had happened leading up to our split said that it probably was her. Maybe she killed herself to show me she wasn't done with terrorizing us."

Jenny laughed gently. "I'd hardly say she was terrorizing us. She sent a few unsettling items, but I'd say that's as far as she would've gone."

Sam made his way into the kitchen and took the whisky out of the alcohol cabinet on the wall. "Do you want one?"

"No, it's a tad early for me. You go ahead; it might help the shock."

He poured the whisky into a glass tumbler and threw it down his throat. It warmed him instantly.

How could Zoe be dead? She was the same age as Sam and had her whole life ahead of her. Surely, she wouldn't want to kill herself over something like this?

"Do you think someone killed her?" Jenny suddenly asked.

"I have no idea, Jenny, and to be honest, I don't want to know. I split from Zoe for a reason, and I still can't get away from her, even though she's dead. I thought I could get over her quickly, and this happens."

They were quiet as Sam poured another whisky into his tumbler, and with curiosity getting the better of him, he wondered if Zoe had been murdered, then who the hell killed her?

They didn't talk about her again for the rest of that day.

13

"So, do you think he killed her?" Lang asked as they sat outside Sam and Jenny's flat.

Preston shook his head. "I don't think so. Did you see his face? He looked like he'd been hit by a truck when we told him."

Lang agreed. He could see it in Sam's eyes that he was no killer. "I'm not so sure about that Jenny—she seemed annoyed at our visit. You think maybe she had something to do with it?"

"No, I don't think Jenny had anything to do with Zoe's death, either. I think she disliked Zoe, for the reasons which she specified. Perhaps she feels differently about her relationship with Sam, and Zoe picked up on it. Maybe Jenny knew this, and that's where the problems started."

Lang shook his head as he reached down for a bottle of water at his feet. "Nah, I don't think so. They're *too* close; their friendship is solid. I think that's probably where the threat lay in Zoe's mind, and that's why she took a dislike to Jenny. Probably didn't want Sam having such a close relationship with another woman, even if it was innocent."

Preston massaged his temples, the stress of the case already getting to him. "You know I love this job, but I can't wait for my retirement next year."

Lang laughed. "You and me both. Before we dream of long days in the sun, we need to get back to Henderson Manor and get a search started, see if we can find anything that points to how she came to her death at the bottom of those stairs."

Preston had already started the car, desperate for the day to be over. "Aye, unfortunately the sun loungers are just out of our reach."

The journey back to the manor was quiet, each officer dreaming of their retirement days. Preston had hoped his last year would be easy; it wasn't looking that way. Glasgow had bred a society of junkies and murderers, and in a lot of cases, each breed of scum had crossed paths. He was sick of dealing with them, but was thankful his days of being a beat officer and having to deal with them in the first instance were far behind him.

Preston sometimes wondered how he had managed to climb the ranks over the years considering that on many occasions he had thought of giving it all up. He had seen people waste away on the streets of Glasgow: junkies lying in shop doors, prostitutes selling themselves to anyone who would take them so they could pay for their next fix, newly legal drinkers getting so drunk they would pass out on the pavement. Yes, he was past all that and was working on finding the real criminals of Glasgow, but he couldn't help wonder where the years had gone and how he had managed to get past all of the grit and grime of the job. Preston knew he was good at his job, but his body was telling him it was time to wind down and make some time for him and the family.

"You good over there, Paul?" Lang interrupted his daydream.

"Eh?"

"You're miles away."

Preston put his dreams of retirement to the back of his mind; he had a while to go before he would be there. They were driving up to the manor, and the forensics team were still in and around the house. "Still busy, I see?"

"Looks like it—maybe they've found something."

Pulling up outside the front door, they could see into the main hallway, and the body of Zoe Henderson lay in its place of death.

"Isn't this job glamorous?" Lang said, with sarcasm.

They entered the hall and took in the surroundings again. The team should have collected most of the evidence they needed to decipher, if the house was a crime scene or the scene of a tragic accident.

One of the head investigators approached Preston and Lang. "Hi, I'm Allan," he said. "I'm head of forensics today, and you'll be glad to know we're almost done here. However, one of our team found something which may be of interest to you both."

"What is it?" Lang asked.

"Follow me," Allan said as he led them up the stairs.

Preston walked up with his back to the wall, trying to see the landing above. "Is it evidence of another person having been here?"

"Not really. We thought you might be able to make more sense of it."

They reached the top of the stairs and were led into a bedroom. It was a large room with almost floor-to-ceiling windows. The air in the room felt heavy.

"So, what did you find?" Lang was becoming impatient.

Allan walked over to the bed and picked up what looked like a shoebox. "All the evidence we need has been taken from this: photographs, fingerprints, and what not. So, you can have it for your part of the investigation. I have to say, some of the things in there are a little strange."

"Can I have a pair of gloves?" Preston asked.

Allan handed him a pair of latex gloves from his forensic suit pocket. "Have a root around in there and tell me if you agree that the contents are slightly odd."

Preston opened the box as Allan held it in his hands, and what he saw confirmed Allan's opinion. "What the hell?"

Allan nodded. "That's what I thought when I saw it."

Preston put the lid back on and looked at Lang, who said nothing. Preston put the lid back on the box, and Allan released it from his grip. "Cheers, we'll get this down to the station and get a proper look."

"I better get back downstairs. See you later."

Preston stayed where he was. He had come to his own conclusions about what had happened to Zoe.

***

"I think we should get Sam Leonard in to have another chat. This confirms a lot of what he and his friend said," Lang said.

They had laid the contents of the box on the table and had examined all of the items. Having heard everything Sam Leonard had said about Zoe Henderson and seeing everything that was inside the box they had collected from the house, Preston and Lang were ninety-nine percent certain of the cause of death. But, to be sure, they would invite Sam into the station to examine the items himself.

"I'll make the call," Preston replied.

"This case could come to a quick close."

Preston nodded as he dialled Sam's number. "Looks like it."

The phone rang for a few moments before it was answered. "Sam? DS Paul Preston here. My colleague and I wondered if you could come into the station. We have something we want to discuss with you."

Preston hung up. "He'll be here within the hour."

Lang gathered the items and placed them back in the shoebox, not wishing Sam to see the evidence before anything had been explained to him. "I'll grab the coffees, then?"

"Any chance of chucking a shot of whisky in mine?" Preston asked.

If they could've gotten away with it, Lang would've used a whole bottle.

14

Sam walked towards the door at Pitt Street station, and if it was possible, his stomach would win gold in the Olympics somersault trials. Various scenarios were going through his head, and he couldn't agree with himself why the police wanted to talk to him again.

He opened the door and stepped inside. Sam had never had any encounters with the police before, and he was worrying about what would happen if the press got wind of the situation. He wasn't *that* famous, but known well enough that if this got out, then it would be all over the Scottish papers before he could blink.

Sam approached the front desk, and suddenly, his throat had become dry. He found himself staring at the officer behind the desk, at a loss for words which would make any sense.

"Can I help you, sir?" the woman asked.

"Erm, yes, I would like to speak to DS Paul Preston. I think he's expecting me."

The female officer smiled. "Your name?"

"Sam Leonard."

"Have a seat please, Mr Leonard. I'll have DS Preston with you in a moment."

Sam sat down on one of the cold, plastic chairs in the waiting area. He felt like a criminal, and his stomach was flipping around so much that he felt like he was going to be sick—again.

"Mr Leonard," Preston's voice boomed. "Glad you could make it in on such short notice. Come this way please."

Sam stood up, wondering if his legs would be able to carry him. "DS Preston, is there something wrong?"

"We have something we would like to show you, and it's important you take the time to study it properly."

Sam felt a wave of confusion wash over him. He found himself in an interview room, and Lang was sat on a chair at the table in the middle.

"Hi."

"Hello, Sam. Thanks for coming in. I presume DS Preston has explained why you're here?" Lang replied.

Sam shook his head. "Not really. All I know is you have something you want to show me. I'm confused… What is it that you have that would concern me?"

Lang glanced at Preston as Sam sat down on the seat opposite. "We do have something to show you. Don't worry because it's nothing sinister. We think you'll understand it and will be able to explain it better than we can."

Sam's hands had become clammy, so he placed them on his knees hoping the denim material would soak up the perspiration. "Can we just get on with it?"

"We went back to the manor house today, and when we arrived, we were handed this by one of the forensics team. What's inside is definitely something you'll want to see."

Sam observed the box with caution, almost like something would jump out and scare him half to death. "What's in it?"

Preston sat down beside Lang. "Open it and have a look. We already have, and it definitely involves you. It was found under Zoe's bed."

Sam wiped his hands on his knees and put on a pair of latex gloves which Preston handed to him. He gripped the lid, and when he lifted it off to look inside, he felt a mixture of shock and sadness. "What's all this?"

"We think that it all links with what you and Jenny were talking about earlier. The hate mail, the photographs, and the phone calls: I think this proves it all."

Sam rose from his chair slowly as he peered into the box of items. He glanced at the two officers. "Can I take them out to get a proper look?"

"Be our guest," Preston replied.

Sam reached in and lifted out a photograph of him with Jenny in a café. "I remember this day; Zoe joined us for some food, and then, Jenny went home. Zoe and I went to the cinema."

Preston and Lang remained silent, which allowed Sam to go through the rest of the box and take it all in.

He took out a number of different photographs and cuttings of Sam's appearances and productions in theatre. He shook his head and sighed as he looked over each item. "I don't understand why she did this."

"Sam, there's more. There was a mobile phone in the box, but we've taken it out and are having it analysed. However, we did have a look at what was on it; can you tell us again what the nature of the text messages and phone calls were?" Preston asked.

"When we got calls, there was never a voice at the other end. But the messages were nasty. Things like, *Jenny is a home wrecker, Sam is taken,* and *Jenny needs to stay away from Sam.* But the worst one said, *If Jenny doesn't move out, something terrible will happen to her.* I was more pissed off than Jenny was about this; she found it funny in the end. She said that it was sad that even though Zoe had me, she still felt the need to be nasty to other women in my life. I thought I could change her behaviour, but this obviously proves she had a vendetta against Jenny."

Preston nodded. "The phone, it had messages on it that fit the description you've given. The prints on the phone match Zoe's, and we just need to link the numbers to prove Zoe was your stalker."

Sam took a deep breath. "I suppose, in a way, I didn't really want to believe it. But this proves she was crazy. She didn't deserve to die, though."

"Who does?" Lang added.

Sam put the items back in the box. "I can't look at this anymore. Do you need anything else from me?"

A gentle tap on the interview room door silenced all three men. Preston got up and opened the door. He paused for a moment and then turned his attention back to Sam.

Watching as Preston sat down opposite him and slid a piece of paper across the table, his stomach lurched once more as he listened. "Any of these look familiar to you?"

Sam studied it carefully. "They're all mine and Jenny's numbers. The messages are the ones that were sent to our phones."

"Sam, you can go now. We won't be needing your assistance any longer."

"Is that it?"

"You told us you ended your relationship with Zoe Henderson because you thought she was stalking you and Jenny, and now we've proved that to be true."

"Thanks for your time."

Sam stood up, not sure how to reply. He left the room and was out of the station quickly. What had just happened? He felt like he had been stabbed in the gut with a blunt knife.

It was ridiculous to feel sad for Zoe after everything he had suspected of her had been confirmed, but he couldn't help it. Was she so alone in that house that when she found love, she felt like she had to fight to keep it? It seemed that way. Their whole relationship had been a lie from day one, and that little shoebox was proof of that.

His thoughts had distracted him from reality, and he found himself outside his front door before he realised where he was. He let himself into the flat.

"Hey, what did they want?" Jenny said as she appeared in the hallway.

"They had a box from Zoe's house."

Jenny frowned. "A box?"

Sam made his way into the kitchen and lifted a beer from the fridge. "Yep, and you want to know what was in it?"

Jenny noted Sam's mixture of emotions. He seemed angry, shocked, drained, and sad. "What?"

"Us!"

"What do you mean us?"

Sam laughed a little; the disbelief of the whole situation seemed funny. "I mean photos, sadistic words on paper of how she hated you and hated me for *not* hating you. And a phone." He gulped on the beer bottle and wished for something stronger.

"What was on it?"

"Only the fucking messages we were getting just before I ended it. I mean, when I ended it, and the messages and the tormenting stopped, I assumed she had decided to leave us alone. But, oh no, she was dead—lying in a heap on the floor in her house on her own, dead."

"What can I do?"

"There's nothing you can do. Looks like Zoe either killed herself, or she fell down those stairs by accident. I don't want to say what I think."

"Just say it. It might make you feel better."

Sam took another gulp of beer. "I ended it, then all of a sudden, she dies. I don't know how soon after, but, Jenny, it makes sense, but it's terrible for me to think she killed herself. I think she threw herself down those stairs on purpose."

Jenny shook her head, "Would she be capable of that, though?"

Sam finished the bottle in his hand. "Deep down, I really didn't think she was capable of doing what she did when we were together; seems like she would do anything to get my attention."

Jenny hugged Sam tightly. "It's over now, though. As awful as it is, she's dead. She can't hurt us anymore."

***

A week after the discovery of the box, Sam had decided it was time to get on with life and forget what had happened. The phone call he had received from DC Lang had helped him to take the first step.

"It seems from the coroner's report and the supporting evidence that Zoe Henderson's death was accidental."

"So that's it done, then?" Sam asked.

"That's it done."

"Thanks, DC Lang."

The conversation was short and fulfilled its purpose. Sam hadn't wished for it to go on any longer than necessary. He didn't want to know anything about a burial or a cremation. He didn't want to hear Zoe Henderson's name ever again.

15

Deborah updated her Facebook status to 'in a relationship.' People would know now he was involved with someone. It would hopefully be enough to warn them off. She wanted Sam to know how she really felt about him, regardless of how complicated things would get. She had no idea he would ever leap into telling her about his past, especially an ex-girlfriend, and so Deborah wanted him to know things about her own life and past in return.

He walked into the pub where they had agreed to meet via text message, and Deborah's heart fluttered. *How can another human being make your heart do that?* She waved him over, trying to avoid spilling the wine on the table as she did so. Her hands were shaking as if she were freezing, but it was the mere thought of his touch that caused it.

"Hello, lovely." His voice floated across the air, reaching her ears with a pleasant buzz. All she could do was smile as he bent down to kiss her on the cheek, sending a ripple across her skin.

"How are you?" she managed.

"I'm fine; however, I do want to talk to you about something."

"Okay," she said, unsure of what to expect.

"Let me get a drink first, I'll be over in a minute." He was back from the bar quickly, holding a whisky tumbler.

"So, what did you want to tell me?" Deborah asked.

Sam took a deep breath before telling her about an ex-girlfriend named Zoe. About how she had been possessive and hated his best friend, Jenny, how she had sent vile messages to the both of them, and how she had handled Sam breaking up with her. How he had worried he wouldn't be able to trust anyone again after what she had done to him, that she had possibly killed herself when he had finally called things off.

"I can't believe you told me all that," Deborah said, feeling exhausted with all of the information.

"Are you glad I told you? Because you can take the time to decide if you really want to carry on with this thing that we have."

Deborah didn't like the sound of the phrase, 'this thing that we have.' Did that mean he was trying to scare her off, and he didn't really want her? Was this his way of telling her he wasn't interested, in the hope she would think it was all too much and would want to leave?

"I'm glad you told me," she managed. There was no way she was going to let him go after all the hard work she had put in to get him. She had made sure she was in the right place at the right time, and even though she had been as nervous as hell, she managed to catch his eye and gathered up his attention. She had allowed herself to go further than anyone else to make sure she got what she wanted; yes, it was a little far-fetched perhaps, but in this day and age, you have to work to get what you want. She had ensured she knew of every theatre date, production, colleague, and anything else she *should* know so she would be in the same place at the same time.

After everything Sam had said about Zoe, he could never know the lengths Deborah had gone to in order to make sure she met him and lured him in with her seductive ways. It would surely freak him out, and he'd would be likely to view her as psychotic, which was the last thing she wanted. She merely put herself into a situation that would work in her favour, that was all; at least that was what she continued to tell herself.

"Do you really believe Zoe was the one who sent all the messages and stuff?" she asked.

"Who else could it have been? It most definitely wasn't Jenny, even if Zoe said it was. Jenny and I have been friends since I can remember; if anything, she would be the one to protect me from psychotic girlfriends."

Deborah nodded as she watched Sam open the bottle of white and pour it into her glass. She listened as it sloshed around inside the glass, realising her brain was probably doing the same thing inside her skull. "I suppose it makes sense. You said she never really liked that your best friend was female."

Sam eyed Deborah as he heard her words, unsure if he should ask his next question. "It doesn't bother you, does it?"

"What? That your best friend is a girl? Come on, Sam. What are we, twelve?" Deborah gave her widest smile. "So, did the police say they would be in touch?" Deborah asked as though she had read his mind.

"There's no need for them to contact me now. It was concluded as accidental death."

Deborah saw his expression deepen again and instantly regretted her question. It was plain to see he was still in shock.

"Why don't we forget about this for now and go back to your place. We could get some Chinese take-out and a bottle of wine?"

Sam smiled, and narrowing his eyes, he replied, "That's what you call it these days?"

Deborah laughed. "All I want is Chinese food and wine. I don't have a clue what you're talking about."

They made their way out of the pub and down the street towards the Chinese takeaway on the corner. Deborah was quiet, thinking about how their relationship might change if the police did conclude Zoe was murdered. They would want to investigate Sam, and anyone else who was involved in Zoe's life. When they found out Sam had a new girlfriend, they would want to talk to her too. Deborah wasn't sure how she would deal with that, if it did happen. She wasn't sure how anyone would deal with it.

***

Sam slid the key into the Yale lock and turned it to the right, allowing the door to click open. The hallway was dark, and the flat was silent as he called out, "Jenny, are you in?" No reply came. "Looks like we have the place to ourselves."

Deborah smiled as she shook her head. "Like I said, it's just Chinese food."

Sam flicked the light switch and was startled to see Jenny standing in the hallway at the entrance to the kitchen. Her hair had fallen over her face, and her eyes were fixed on Sam and Deborah. "Jesus, Jenny, you scared us half to death."

Jenny didn't reply; she didn't move. She cocked her head to one side, focusing her stare on Deborah through the strands of hair in front of her eyes. She smiled slightly, her teeth not showing as they hid behind her dried-out lips.

"Jenny, are you all right?" Sam asked, placing the takeout bag on the floor by his feet.

Jenny did not reply to his question. Instead, she kept her gaze on Deborah, who had taken a step behind Sam and was holding his hand. "Sam, what's wrong with her?" she whispered.

Sam broke his grip from Deborah's hand and took a few steps towards Jenny. He put his hand on her shoulder, and she turned to face him. Sam noted Jenny didn't look well—her face had turned almost grey, and her lips were dry and cracked. "Jenny, what's wrong?"

She lifted her head, hair falling from her face to reveal eyes which showed no life within them. "Hello, Sam." Jenny's voice was hoarse with a hint of playfulness behind it.

Sam looked over to Deborah, who had stepped backwards closer to the front door. "I think she's sleepwalking."

"Has she done this before?"

"Once or twice, when I was with Zoe; I think its stress related." He placed his hands gently on Jenny's shoulders and guided her into her bedroom. "Take the food into the kitchen, will you, Deborah? I'll be with you in a minute."

Deborah nodded as she picked up the bag and walked cautiously into the kitchen. She froze when she heard Jenny say, "Goodnight, Deborah."

The sound of her voice sent chills up her spine. "Goodnight, Jenny," she replied, trying not to allow the fear to come across in her voice.

She heard Sam close the bedroom door, and soon, he was behind her in the kitchen. He nuzzled her neck and wrapped his hands around her waist. "Do you want to skip the food?"

"Actually, no. I'm quite hungry as it happens."

Sam laughed quietly. "So, are you thinking food, then...?" The question hung in the air.

"I'm thinking that you don't ever give up, do you?" Deborah turned to face him and jumped as she saw Jenny in the hallway again.

"Hey, you two. I could smell the food, and I'm sorry to say I'm a weakling when it comes to Chinese... Any going spare?" Jenny asked, with chirpiness in her voice.

Sam spun around, surprised to hear Jenny out of bed. "I've just put you to bed."

"Sorry?" Jenny said.

"Yeah, you were sleep walking again."

Jenny shook her head. "I haven't done that for a while."

Sam nodded. "You want some rice and chicken balls? We ordered too much."

Deborah wasn't enamoured that, yet again, she and Sam had been interrupted. Jenny wasn't as annoying as Deborah had first anticipated, but she still didn't appreciate this second interruption.

"You don't mind, do you, Deborah?" Jenny asked.

Deborah smiled as she shook her head. "Like Sam said, we ordered too much. In fact, why don't we go and work up an appetite so we can *really* enjoy this food?"

Jenny's eyes widened at Deborah's audacity. "I'll eat this in the living room." She left the kitchen and Sam and Deborah alone, not wanting to intrude when Deborah had clearly stated what was on her mind. The boldness of some people.

"You said you were hungry." Sam smiled.

Deborah reached up and kissed Sam's lips gently. "I *am* hungry."

Sam reached down and took her hand in his and led her to his bedroom. She sat down on the bed, removing her shoes. "You said you thought it was stress related?"

"I think so. She'd never done it before Zoe and isn't aware if she did it as a child. It was when Zoe was sending those messages, the endless photographs of us together, the letters. I hated it; she wore us both down. She swore it wasn't her, and for a while, I think I believed her. That was when Jenny started sleep walking."

Deborah held out her hand. "Come here."

He went to her, allowing himself to flop down beside her. "You're pretty amazing, do you know that?"

She smiled, feeling flattered by the compliment. "I am?"

"What kind of girl sticks around after finding out about all of my baggage?"

Deborah stood up and removed her dress, exposing her body. "I didn't find out; you told me about it. And while we're on the subject, I'm not a girl but a woman who knows her own mind."

Sam placed a hand on either side of Deborah's waist. "I do like a woman who knows her own mind."

Deborah allowed Sam to let go of his worries, but she knew there was a very strong possibility this would have to end at some point. But for the time being, she drank in every ounce of Sam Leonard she could.

16

Sam snored softly as he lay in Deborah's arms. She could smell the coconut shampoo in his hair, and she let the scent fill her lungs. Had she fallen in love with him? She was quite certain she had; not surprising really, considering the lengths she had gone to, to be with him. Deborah had followed everything Sam had done over the last two years, at first due to a genuine interest in his work. But then, something triggered inside her, something deep within she couldn't explain, and she knew from the moment she saw him in the flesh on the stage, she couldn't get enough of him. Deborah was aware it would be a long shot that he would even consider going on a date with her, so when he offered to buy her a drink the night of the closing show, her heart had risen into her throat.

She watched his chest rise and fall as he breathed softly in his slumber, unaware of all the things in her head. Sam could never know; it would ruin everything for everyone. He was so beautiful; conscious or otherwise, his skin was perfectly soft, and to her, he was precious. As Deborah continued to admire Sam, she heard footsteps outside in the hallway. She sighed, wondering if Jenny was sleepwalking again and hoped she wasn't. It had freaked her out the way Jenny stared at them both through the gaps in her hair. It was like she was reading Deborah's mind, which, of course, wasn't possible, but it scared her all the same. The footsteps had turned to a shuffle and were loud at times and quiet at others. If Deborah didn't know any better, she would say Jenny was trying to scare her on purpose. She snuggled down under the duvet and cuddled into Sam. His skin on hers made her feel warm and tingly.

Suddenly, there was a loud thud outside the bedroom door, and the sound of Jenny's screams pierced Deborah's ears. Sam sat up and was out of the bed before Deborah realised.

"What the hell was that?" he asked.

"I think it was Jenny."

Deborah followed him. She watched as he kneeled down beside Jenny and brushed her hair out of her face. "Jenny, can you hear me?"

"I'll phone for an ambulance," Deborah said, trying to mute her panic.

Jenny wasn't moving. She *was* breathing, but she seemed lifeless. Sam moved her into the recovery position and ran back into his bedroom to retrieve a blanket to cover her. "Jenny, I'm here. We're getting you an ambulance."

"It's on its way." Deborah placed her hand on Sam's shoulder. "I'll stay here until you get some clothes on, and then, I'll get dressed."

"Okay, I'll be two minutes."

As Sam dressed himself in the bedroom, Deborah stroked Jenny's hair and stayed by her side. She knew she shouldn't, but for some reason, she couldn't help but feel excited at what had happened. She tried to push the feelings to the back of her head. She didn't want those kinds of thoughts invading her mind again. "You do like to make a fuss, don't you, Jenny. First, the sleepwalking and now this; you'll have Sam worried sick." Her voice was soft, as if she were speaking to a new-born baby.

Sam was once again beside Jenny. "Quickly get dressed so that we can go with the ambulance."

Deborah smiled inwardly but didn't dare show it. "They'll only let one of us in with her. You go. I'll go home, and you can phone me later to let me know how she's doing."

Sam frowned. "You're not coming to the hospital?"

"Of course I'll come. I'll get a taxi."

The buzzer rang out louder than usual, perhaps because the night carried such stillness, everything sounded louder when the world was sleeping. Sam got up and pressed the release button, and in seconds, the paramedics were in the flat. Sam explained what had happened, and before Deborah could blink, Jenny was on a stretcher, and Sam was shoving a set of keys in her hand. "Lock up for us, please. We're going to the Western Infirmary. I'll meet you there."

He was gone, and in an instant, the flat was empty. Deborah went into Sam's room to retrieve her bag and made sure all of the lights were out. She proceeded to close the door, and as she did, she felt a presence behind her. She turned, but of course nothing faced her.

She closed the door and put the key in the lock, turning it once and trying the handle to make sure she had locked it properly. On trying the handle, she was shocked at how cold it had suddenly become.

As Deborah headed for the stairs, she pretended to herself she couldn't hear the low growl coming from Sam and Jenny's flat.

***

On her arrival at the hospital, Deborah was met with the usual A&E suspects: drunks, drug addicts, and street brawlers. She sometimes really did hate Glasgow, but now that she had met Sam, the place had become a little brighter, even that night. Deborah took her phone out and sent a text message to Sam.

I'm here, where are you? Is Jenny okay?

On pressing 'send,' she looked up at the main entrance to the A&E department. There was an old man outside smoking a cigarette, and he was clutching a walking stick. She thought of her granddad and decided to check if the man was okay. She approached him, and he was clearly unaware he had caught her interest.

"Are you okay?" she asked gently.

The man looked up on hearing Deborah's voice. "Aye, hen, thanks." Smoke filtered from his mouth as he spoke. On seeing that she wasn't satisfied with his answer, he went on.

"My granddaughter fell down the stairs tonight, broke her bloody ankle, so she did. It's a bad one, too, all puffed up an' that."

Deborah gave a sympathetic smile. "I'm sure she'll be okay, especially if she has you here."

He returned the smile. "Aye, hen, she will that. She's tough as auld boots, my Zoe. Nothing phases her."

Deborah felt the bile rise at the sound of his granddaughter's name, and it must have shown.

"Are you a'right, love? You've went an awful funny colour, so ye have." The man braced himself against his walking stick as he stood up straight, stepping on his cigarette.

Deborah swallowed hard. "I'm fine, thank you. It's just that… well, my partner's friend collapsed tonight, and I'm not so sure if she'll be okay."

At that, Sam came out from the swinging doors of the entrance. "There you are. She's awake."

Deborah looked at the man with sad eyes. He smiled at her. "Your friend must be as tough as my Zoe."

Sam was already pulling her inside. "Thanks," Deborah mouthed as she entered the hospital. Was that guilt that ran through her veins at the mere mention of Zoe's name? Obviously, it wasn't *the* Zoe, but hearing the name and that she had fallen down the stairs was enough to make Deborah's stomach lurch. She was pulled back from her thoughts when she realised Sam was talking to her.

"The doctor wants to do some routine blood tests."

Deborah nodded. "And what will that tell us?"

Sam shook his head. "Hopefully, nothing. Maybe she was sleepwalking again, you know, after she'd gone back to bed."

Deborah hoped that was all it was; you didn't faint for no reason. "Can that happen?"

Deborah hadn't realised it but she and Sam had been walking along the corridor and had made their way into the ward. She was suddenly standing in Jenny's cubicle, by her bed. "Oh, you're awake. How are you feeling?"

Jenny smiled weakly. "I'm not sure. I don't feel *great*."

Sam was at her side, with Jenny's hand in his. Deborah's heart ached on seeing Sam so hurt.

"You didn't have to come here. You could've both stayed at home." Jenny's voice was weak. Her eyes scrunched at the pain in her stomach.

"What? You want me to call a doctor?" Sam panicked.

Jenny shook her head. "It could be food poisoning. I was sick earlier, after that bloody Chinese."

Deborah approached the other side of the bed. "You did get out of bed to eat it. Maybe your stomach couldn't handle it sitting in there once you'd fallen asleep again."

Jenny's brow furrowed. "Erm, since when did you become a nutrition specialist?" She laughed quietly.

A nurse came into the cubicle. "I need to take some blood. Could you wait outside, please?"

Sam and Deborah did as they were asked, Deborah quite happily; she hated needles. "It probably is food poisoning. She had the chicken balls, and we didn't."

Sam nodded. "That's true. It was just scary seeing her there, lifeless on the floor."

Deborah was hugging him now, wanting to take away the pain he felt for his friend, but at the same time wanting nothing more than to be alone with him. "She'll probably get kept in overnight. They'll want to make sure everything's fine, and with it being a Saturday, they probably won't get the results straight away."

The nurse opened the cubicle curtain and stepped out. "You can go back in now."

Jenny had her eyes closed and seemed peaceful, her chest rising and falling slowly.

"We shouldn't wake her," Sam said.

"I'm not asleep but almost. Go home and come back tomorrow," Jenny said softly.

"That's me told, then," Sam laughed.

He kissed her on the forehead, and Deborah didn't look. She couldn't look; it was too hard to see him be that way with her. Deborah knew she was being unreasonable, and that he loved Jenny purely as a friend, but she couldn't help but feel like he was becoming hers, only hers.

"We'll be back tomorrow, first thing," Deborah said. She wanted Jenny to know she would be looked after, but she also wanted her to be aware Sam wouldn't be alone.

They left, hand in hand, and made their way out to the main road. The street was quiet; the pubs and clubs had closed two hours previously, and the only life on the street was the ambulance workers going in and out of the hospital. Sam flagged down a passing taxi, and they got in.

"Palazzo Apartments on Ingram Street, please, mate," Sam said.

The taxi driver nodded and pulled out onto the road. They were silent on the way back to Sam and Jenny's flat, and Deborah wondered if she would hear that low growl again once Sam fallen asleep.

She sincerely hoped that she wouldn't. Someone knew something about her which she did not want Sam to find out about. She would do anything to stop that from happening.

17

Jodie smiled as Patrick held a protective hand over her pregnant belly. They stood still, looking up at the house. It was marvellous, with a hedge growth that reached the height of the large windows at the front.

"I can't *believe* this is our home." Jodie smiled.

"I know, a new start for all three of us," Patrick replied, with a boyish grin.

Jodie turned to face him, and she saw a twinkle in his eye. "Shall we go in, then?"

Patrick nodded and handed over the keys to the front door. Jodie felt the baby flutter as she put the key inside the lock. She took it as a good sign; this was going to be a wonderful place to start their new lives and bring up their first child. After everything that had happened in the last two years, they both deserved it.

She opened the door and stood still, looking into the entrance hallway, and she drank in the view. The place certainly needed sprucing up a little but that didn't matter. The house was huge with old-fashioned carpets and high ceilings. "I love it already." Jodie had viewed the brochure pictures from the auction, but she hadn't viewed the house properly.

"Come on, I'll show you the sitting room." He pulled her hand gently and led her into the room on the right-hand side of the hallway.

The room was large, enough space for a dining table to fit eight around it, plus a three-piece suite and still have plenty of room left over. The window was centred at the bottom of the room and stretched from two feet off the floor, almost all the way up to the ceiling. The natural light from outside gave the room a pretty glow which matched Jodie's mood and appearance.

"Come on, the kitchen is huge. You'll love it in there." Patrick was pulling her once more.

"Hey, you cheeky bugger, just because I'm the woman?" she joked.

Patrick led her down the hallway and through an arched doorway. He was right—she did love it. The kitchen ceiling was so high that there was no way she would be able to reach it, even standing on a chair. The large decorative light that hung down was beautiful, with butterfly-shaped glass around each bulb. It did need a good dust and polish, but Jodie had no clue how she would be able to do that with the height it hung from. Patrick stole her attention away from the dusty glass butterflies and beckoned her to the large door at the end of the kitchen.

"Your outdoor space, madam." Patrick opened the door, and natural light flooded the kitchen. The garden was partly paved with large neutral-coloured concrete slabs, running from the door to the middle of the garden. Jodie could see a small pond in the far right corner, leading her to realise the other half of the garden was covered in a healthy green grass, overgrown, yes, but healthy looking.

"This will be perfect for our little one here," she said, patting her stomach gently.

"It sure will."

Jodie felt her eyes sting, but refused to allow any tears to fall. Patrick wasn't blind or deaf, and though he could hear her thoughts, she knew he would never invade her privacy by speaking out. "What's wrong?"

Jodie took a breath. "Nothing. I'm just feeling a little overwhelmed by it all. I mean, if you had told me two years ago this was where we would be, a beautiful new home and a baby on the way, I wouldn't have believed it."

The last two years had been a mental struggle for Jodie. After the Ross situation, she had decided to lay off the psychic scene for a while and had taught herself to tune out from her ability, for two reasons. One, she knew if she didn't, it would slowly drive her insane; the last time had almost killed her and sent her mind into darker places than she could have imagined possible. Two, if she and Patrick were serious about starting a family, then that was all she wanted to focus on, and she didn't want anything getting into her mind-set and screwing it up for her. Jodie would never speak ill of the dead, but in her eyes, there was more to life than death. Of course, she still liked she had this ability—after all, it had prevented more deaths two years earlier. But she knew for the sake of her future and mental health, she could never go back there.

"I know. But we're here now, aren't we?" Patrick stroked her hair.

Jodie smiled.

"Why don't you go upstairs and check out the rest of the rooms, and you can decide which one will be the baby's. I'll go out to the car and grab our cases, and then, we can unload the van."

"Okay." Jodie nodded as she watched Patrick head back to the front door. She closed the door to the view of the perfect garden and headed to the main hallway. Patrick had left the front door open, and she could see him at the van, unloading the cases. Jodie turned her back to the open door and faced the stairway which led to the upper level of the house.

She placed her hand on the rail on the left-hand side and began the climb. Being eight and a half months pregnant did tend to take its toll when climbing a large, old fashioned staircase, and she quickly realised this. The stairs reached a turn three-quarters of the way up, and she was thankful when she saw there were only another three steps after the bend.

"Right, now that I've conquered Mount Everest, I can find your room," Jodie spoke down to her bump. She only had to take three steps forward before she came to the first room, which was on her left. She opened the door and found that it was dark and a little stale. "Oh God, I wonder how long these windows have been closed for."

She flipped the switch, but light did not fill the room. She sighed and made her way in to find the window. She opened the large, heavy curtains, lifted the safety latch, and pushed the window up to let in some fresh air. Something bright caught her eye. A yellow teddy bear sat perched on the window ledge. Jodie reached over and lifted it. Its fur was soft but its appearance was old, the paws were a little tattered and the stitching on one of the arms had come a little loose.

"God knows how long you've been here, you look ancient." Jodie said.

She turned back to face the room, holding the bear close to her chest. There was a mountain of space, and she was almost certain this was the room for the baby. Jodie looked up and could see there were cobwebs in the corners of the ceiling, and some of the paper was coming away from the top of the walls. That wouldn't be a problem, because they would be redecorating anyway. Jodie considered how small her newborn would be and how many clothes they would come to have, piles of toys and book would line the shelves she imagined Patrick would put on the walls. Then, she thought about all the things she still had to buy and the little time they actually had left. She smiled as she made her way down the hall to explore the next room.

"This can be the guest room."

It was a little smaller than the last. It didn't have as much space, but was still bigger than any room in the flat at Glasgow Harbour. More cobwebs lingered in the corners, and there were a few cracks in the old paint job. Goodness knows the last time it had been decorated.

She passed the bathroom, which was old and in desperate need of a white suite and new tiles. It would be too big a job for them to do with the baby coming and trying to settle in, so they would get someone in to do it. Jodie pictured what she wanted in their new bathroom as she glanced whilst making her way down toward the last room, which faced her head on.

She opened the door and was surprised to find that the removal people hadn't touched this room. It looked lived in but tidy.

The bed was neat, as though someone had only just made it. The window was dressed symmetrically, just how Jodie would have dressed it. She walked in and opened one of the drawers in the large dresser to find clothes inside.

"Great, another job to add to the list." She sighed.

Jodie closed the drawer and walked over to the dressing table that still harboured perfume bottles and the odd scented candle.

"Patrick?" Jodie looked out of the large bay window in the centre of the back wall to see if he was still outside unloading the van. She could see he was struggling with a large box which was labelled 'bedroom.'

Jodie smiled and turned to go back downstairs when she heard a large thud coming from the hallway. Thinking Patrick had come into the house and dropped the box, she quickly moved to the top of the stairs, where she found nothing. She could hear Patrick's footsteps on the gravel outside, which would mean she was the only one inside the house. She shrugged it off, putting it down to the house being old and unoccupied for quite some time.

"Patrick, do you need a hand?"

Patrick looked up. "No, I'm fine. I want to get the necessities in before it gets dark, and then, I can get the rest done tomorrow." He dropped the box gently, inside the front door.

"Okay, well, I've picked the baby's room."

"Great." He seemed distant.

Jodie thought about all they had been through and how Patrick had been the one to hold it together when she had struggled. And now, they were having a baby and moving into their new home.

"You okay?"

"Yes, just thinking about the baby's room. So, you want to show me and tell me your ideas?"

Jodie led Patrick upstairs and noted how quiet he had become. "What's wrong?"

"I keep thinking about him, about what he did to us," Patrick replied. "I know I shouldn't. But I'm still angry about what happened."

"This is our fresh start, Patrick. You don't have to waste your energy on him anymore. He's gone. He can't hurt us anymore."

"I know. Sometimes he creeps into my head before I've even realised it," Patrick replied before gesturing to the yellow bear Jodie was still clutching. "Where'd you get that?"

"I found it in the baby's room. He's really old by the looks of him. He was on the window when I opened the curtains. I think he's been here for years."

"Must've been. Apparently the same family have owned this place for years."

Jodie looked down at the bear. "I'm going to fix him up, clean him, and sew his arm back on. I know it sounds weird, but I feel like he belongs here."

"Doesn't sound weird at all," Patrick replied.

Scraping and creaking sounded above them as they reached the top of the stairs. It distracted Jodie from their conversation. "Do you hear that noise? I thought it was maybe a mouse or a bird when I heard it earlier."

"Yeah, I hear it. Can't think what else it could be."

Jodie's brow creased, and then, she smiled. "You seriously believe that's all it is?"

"Why not? Not every noise is a ghost, Jodie."

She paused for a moment more, uncertain as to whether he was genuine or trying to protect her from the ability she didn't want to face for the time being. She considered the latter for a brief moment and then let it fall out of her head. "So, are you ready to see this little one's room?" she asked as she opened the door, desperate to continue the distraction and bring Patrick back from reliving their hell.

"More than ready."

Jodie watched as her husband looked around, taking in the surroundings.

"You know, we'll never have to move again. We're set for life here," said Patrick as he pictured where the cot would go.

"I know, it's amazing. I'm so glad you found this place."

18

"I've been looking forward to this all day," Jodie said as she put the food onto the plates.

"Have you?"

"It's all this unpacking malarkey; it's given this baby a big appetite."

Patrick smiled as he took in his new surroundings. The kitchen was so big, and he knew that it would be cold in the winter time. He watched as Jodie popped the first chip into her mouth. "Good?"

"Mmm, you have no idea." She smiled.

They made their way over to the large table situated at the back of the kitchen, near to the back door. "I think I would like to move this away because it will be cold to sit near there in the winter," said Jodie.

"Yeah, I think so too."

They ate in silence, happily going over the events of the day. It had been a very busy day moving boxes and furniture. The opportunity to buy the house had come at a time which was almost perfect for them. The church had been doing well, and the cottage at Lomond Park, inherited from Patrick's aunts, had been accommodated every week for the last two years, so money was in no way tight. Patrick's parents had also kept by a legal document, which had only to be issued once Patrick was married. He had known about it, and that it had been kept under wraps for years after his parents had passed away, and his understanding was he wouldn't be made aware of what the purpose of the document was until he was married. After the wedding, both Patrick and Jodie had forgotten about it, considering everything that had happened in the run up to the wedding.

Patrick had found his brother in the same instant he watched him die, and to top it off, had solved Glasgow's first murder investigation involving a serial killer, and he had also watched his fiancée go through hell as he tried to do so, so his mind couldn't have been further from a mystery legal document.

However, when they did remember about it a few months after their lives had settled down to normality again, Patrick was a little unsure whether or not he wanted to revisit his parents' deaths once again. He had taken a long time to move on from their tragedy, and if it hadn't have been for Jodie, then he was certain that he wouldn't be here today. Going back to the lawyer to go over legalities of it was the last thing he wanted to do; it would bring back the pain from the first time around. Having to go through their personal things and all of their finances, he hadn't wanted to face it again. Jodie had convinced him to, as she was able to do with most things, and after several signatures on various documents, a sum of fifty thousand pounds was paid into Patrick's joint account with Jodie. To say he had been shocked was an understatement.

It had been quite simple considering the amount of money his parents had left for them. Patrick wasn't made aware of where the money had come from. Had it been an estate or savings his parents had been putting away in secret? He didn't know. All the same, he couldn't have been more grateful.

They had celebrated quietly with a bottle of champagne and a three-course meal in a restaurant in Byres Road, a nice little Italian with low lighting and a grand piano in the corner. Patrick and Jodie had discussed what to do with the money and had decided upon a new home, since they had been trying for a family.

They had searched for a few months, finding houses that were nice but nothing spectacular. Then, Patrick had come across 'Henderson Manor.' Not quite a manor in this day and age, but in its early days, certainly a manor house. The brochure hadn't done it much justice but enough to catch Patrick's eye.

He had kept it a secret from Jodie until he knew for sure it was where he wanted to be. He knew deep down she would love it.

It was being auctioned for a lot less than it was worth due to the fact the family who had resided there for over a century no longer existed. The last member of the bloodline had passed away suddenly, and there was no named person in the legal documents to take the house. The last member of that family hadn't drawn up a will, so the house was taken to auction. Patrick didn't understand the whole legal process, but he didn't care. All he wanted was to see it for himself.

Having gone to see the house, he could see it really had been a home for a lot of people from the same family. The house was huge, and Patrick could feel the history once he stepped inside it for the first time. The staircase in the front hall way creaked in a way that said many, many people had used them. There was an outhouse Patrick was told was used as a wash and laundry facility. On hearing this, he understood how long the house had been standing for. The auctioneer had said the property had belonged to one family since the early 1800s. The front entrance to the grounds of the house displayed large sandstone walls, and the two front pillars had 'Henderson Manor' engraved into them.

"It makes it sound a little creepy, like something you'd find in a horror film," Patrick had said to the auctioneer. Patrick made him aware he wasn't at all spooked by the house, and that he was making a passing judgment.

On his entrance to the grounds, the stones crunched under his shoes, and the fir trees that surrounded the grounds blew gently in the wind. Before he was even inside, he knew this was the house he wanted to spend his life in with Jodie and their new addition. The house was in a position where they could move in immediately and make the changes they wanted while living there. Patrick was determined, and it paid off as he was successful at the auction.

"Are you glad we found it?" Patrick broke the happy silence.

"I couldn't be happier if I tried. It's amazing."

"I don't know why I asked you that — I know you're happy."

Later, Jodie went out with the rubbish bag, leaving Patrick to clean the kitchen. She could feel herself waddle as she moved.

What are you doing to me, little one? she thought as she opened the back door. She could hear Patrick washing the dishes as she went outside. The grounds were dark until a security light lit up the whole area, allowing her to see into the fir trees and over to an area she hadn't had the chance to look at since moving in. She placed the rubbish into the bin and walked across the gravel and stones to the back end of the house.

As she drew closer, she slowed her pace, unsure if her eyes were playing tricks on her. Her brow furrowed, almost like she was trying to see more clearly. Eventually, she realised what she thought she had seen was entirely correct.

Henderson Family
Here we lay together not able to go on
We trust in you to stay together
And keep the family strong
We worked hard everyday
To get to where we are
Our family ties will keep us together
For we are never really far.

Here lies

Edith Henderson
1871-1949
A loving wife to Walter and mother to George

Walter Henderson
1870-1950
A loving husband to Edith and father to George

George Henderson
1896-1970
A loving husband to Anna and father to Audrey

Anna Henderson
1898-1970
A loving wife and mother

Audrey Henderson
1957-1982
A loving wife to James and mother to Zoe

James Henderson
1953-2002
A loving husband to Audrey and father to Zoe

Helen Henderson
1921-2008
Wife, mother and grandmother

"What?" Jodie whispered. She stared at the burial plots that were in her garden. "Is this a joke?" she asked, louder this time. She turned, half marching, half waddling back into the kitchen where Patrick was tidying up.

"You didn't get lost, then?" He smiled.

"No, no, I didn't get lost, but I did find something rather interesting." She returned the smile sarcastically.

"What is it?"

"You mean, you didn't know there are gravestones on our property?"

Patrick smiled. "Oh, that. I thought there was something wrong."

Jodie couldn't believe how calm he was. "What do you mean, 'oh, that'? Patrick, there are *gravestones,* burial plots, on our new property!"

Patrick took her hand and led her to the kitchen table. "Did you read them?"

"Yes, there are bloody seven of them under there." Her head was in her hands.

"What's wrong? It's only a few memorials of the people who used to live here. The first man to have gone in there was born over one hundred years ago, in this house, by all accounts. I think it's a nice history to come with the place. Come on, there had to be something to come from a house this old. It gives it character."

Jodie nodded, knowing he was right. But she still couldn't believe that there were dead people in her garden. "Yes, but I didn't actually think we'd get the history *and* the remains."

Patrick laughed. "Hardly. Come on, Jodie. You of all people should know this isn't going to turn into a zombie fest. It's just that, the family who owned this 'manor,' as they named it, wanted the family history to stay here as long as possible. Each one of them lived here, reared their children here and died here. They ran a whisky firm by all accounts, Henderson Whisky, funnily enough."

Jodie rolled her eyes. She knew there was nothing scary about death, yet she was still surprised there were graves in her garden. "I know. So long as we don't end up in there, that's all I care about."

Patrick smiled. "Very funny. Come on. Let's get up and unpack our bedding. I'm done for the day."

"And if you hear from any one of them, keep it to yourself. I'd rather not be aware of an old spirit wandering around our house while I'm in the bath." Jodie was laughing; however, she wasn't joking. She really didn't want to know about anything spiritual until the baby was born. She didn't need the stress. Remembering how ill it made her when Patrick was working alongside the police while Ross was going around strangling people made her shiver. She didn't want to become ill with stress when she was pregnant with her first child.

"I won't say a word."

As they climbed the stairs to their new bedroom, both were unaware of the presence already appearing before them. Edith Henderson knew Patrick was the only person who would be able to help her and the rest of the Henderson family bring home what was rightfully theirs.

19

The gravel was surprisingly smooth yet cold on his bare feet as he made his way across the grounds, towards the Henderson memorial plot. He had decided to call it a memorial plot, rather than graves or burial plot. Even though having them on the grounds of his house didn't bother him, he still would rather Jodie felt comfortable in her own home. So, if that meant changing the way they referred to it, then that was what they would do.

He found he was walking slowly and realised his legs felt as if they were full of lead. His eyes were focused on the memorial plot, and he was aware he felt worried, but he couldn't figure out why.

Help us!

Patrick stopped when he heard it – a female voice that sounded frail and distant. He continued to walk, again feeling as though he was fighting against a force pushing him back. But he wouldn't give in. Something was telling him he had to get to the side of the memorial plot.

She's missing, came another voice, a man this time, still frail but not as distant.

Patrick tried to focus on his goal. He put all of his energy into taking one step further, and by the time he reached the plot, he felt physically drained. What he didn't expect to see was what shocked him more than the struggle to get there. The plot was empty. He could see the plot was actually split into three sections, and all of them were empty. Patrick wasn't scared of spirits, but he had never experienced a situation where bodies had gone missing before. And not just any body, bodies that were meant to be buried at his house. He was nervous to look around and find all seven spirits standing there, waiting for him.

"Who are you referring to?" he asked aloud, hoping to get a name. However, he wasn't so sure a name would help; the family had been here for over a century.

We should be together, came the first voice again.

Patrick wondered if he had the strength for another spiritual mystery. The last one had almost sent Jodie over the edge with panic attacks and sleep deprivation. He couldn't afford any of that to happen now.

"I had to pick a haunted house, didn't I?" he said as he turned to face the house, fully expecting an audience. When he didn't find one, he decided to go back inside. The security light flickered, and before it went out completely, Patrick felt a coldness creep over him. The hairs on his body stood on end, and he shivered, realising that, for some reason, he was only wearing a pair of boxers and a T-shirt.

He felt a cold hand place itself upon his right shoulder as the light went off, and he turned around startled to find the face of an old woman so close to him that, had she been alive, he would have felt her breath on his face.

Help us find her!

Patrick found himself alone in the rear grounds of the house, cold and with sore feet. He looked for the woman who had appeared to him. She was nowhere around. When he thought about it, he couldn't remember why he was outside in the first place. All he could think of was he was trying to get to the memorial plot and it had taken all his strength. His legs no longer felt heavy, so he walked over to the plot, remembering it had been open and empty. He approached with caution only to find everything as it should be. The plots were not open and certainly not empty.

Patrick looked up at the clear sky and breathed a sigh of relief. "I was sleepwalking." He couldn't understand it, even though he was relieved it was all a dream. He hadn't done it since he was little. He went back inside as soon as he realised he was outside in the middle of the night, semi-naked.

As he entered the kitchen, Jodie came in through the hall's entrance. "What are you doing?" she asked as she rubbed her eyes.

"I was bloody sleepwalking. I woke up outside," he replied as he shook his head in confusion.

"You haven't done that since you were little."

"You're telling me. Don't know what that's all about."

Jodie filled the kettle. "So, I can't sleep, and you're walking around half asleep. Fancy a cuppa?"

Patrick nodded. "I'll go up and get some clothes on; it's a bit chilly out there."

Jodie laughed. "You will be cold, if you're wandering around outside in your boxer shorts."

As he made his way up to their bedroom, Patrick couldn't help but think there was a meaning behind the dream. It had felt very real to him, and he couldn't help but think whatever the meaning of it was, it had led him out to the memorial plot. And those voices, they were so real, full of passion. They had been looking for someone. Someone they claimed was missing, but missing from where?

Patrick entered the bedroom and pulled on a pair of tracksuit bottoms and put on a pair of thick socks to warm his toes. He walked over to the window and looked out over the front entrance of the manor. He scanned the long, gravel-covered drive and noticed the front gates were open. Patrick was quite sure he had closed them.

Help us find her, was whispered into his ear. He jumped not only at the voice but also at the reflection in the window. Patrick spun around, but there was no one behind him. He realised he had been right; the dream did mean something, and it *had* led him out to the plot. Patrick decided he would communicate and find out who exactly was contacting him and why. But not now; it was too soon.

"We've only just moved in, for God's sake."

He switched off from the connection and went down to join his wife for a cup of tea, leaving the spirits of goodness knows who to wait until he was ready for them. Patrick really hadn't expected something to come up in the house, or at least not so soon. He didn't want Jodie to know, so he kept it to himself, allowing her to enjoy the pregnancy in peace.

As he entered the kitchen, he found Jodie had already made his tea and had laid his mug on the kitchen table, across from where she was sitting. "So…barefoot?

Patrick shook his head. "I know. I haven't a clue why, maybe because we're in a new house on the first night. Maybe my mind was trying to work its way around the place while I slept."

Jodie knew there was something he wasn't telling her, and she was a little pissed off he was keeping it from her. "You said this was a fresh start for us."

Patrick looked up, uncomfortable with the indirect approach she had taken for what she really wanted to say. "It *is* a fresh start." His throat was beginning to dry up; she really did know how to get his pulse racing.

"Then why the lies?" She was smiling a little.

"Lies?"

"Why were you really out there? I believe you were sleepwalking, but I don't believe you when you say you don't know the reason." Jodie tapped the mug with her index finger, the nail creating a *ding* sound against the porcelain.

"It's nothing for you to worry about. I can handle whatever it is that's going on here by myself."

"So, there is something going on?"

He looked down at her bump, knowing that any potential stress could be harmful to their baby. Patrick certainly didn't want to be the one who put his baby or wife in harm's way. "Like I said, nothing for you to worry about."

"You said that the last time. It was something you and the police would work on, and I didn't have to worry. Then look what happened; I almost died. I don't know about you, but I don't want anything like that to happen ever again, especially now we're going to be parents."

"I'm serious. If you don't want to worry, then I don't have to tell you."

"Patrick, that's ridiculous. You're my husband, and this is our new home. If there is something happening here, I want to know about it."

Patrick knew this was leading to an argument, and either way, Jodie would be the one who suffered from it. If he didn't tell her, then she would be angry at him for keeping it from her, and if he did tell her what happened out at the plots, then she would worry about the effect it would have on him and their relationship, not to mention the baby. "I'm torn whether to tell you or not."

"So, tell me. You know it's a strain if you don't."

"You're sure you want to know? Earlier today, you said you'd rather not know," Patrick pressed, willing her to change her mind.

She nodded, showing him that no amount of stalling would make her rethink.

"Okay, I'll tell you." Patrick moved around to the same side of the table as Jodie; he wasn't so sure why he did this, but he felt it necessary. "I was led out there, to be shown something."

"Shown what?"

"The plot outside; when I got out there, in my head, the plot was open."

"In your *head* it was open?"

"Yes, but not only that, the plot was empty. There were no bodies inside."

Jodie shook her head. "You're sure about this?"

"I was told that there is someone missing from it. That I had to help find her, that they should all be together."

Jodie took his hand, "Who's missing?"

"I have no idea."

20

Patrick stood by Jodie as they both looked down at their baby boy, who was sound asleep. The yellow teddy bear had been placed at the bottom of the cot. They had decided the bear needed some attention, and once they'd fixed it up, they agreed it would be their baby's first comforter.

"I can't believe he's mine!" Jodie said as she stared down at their son.

"Ours." Patrick smiled.

Jodie nodded. "Yes, of course, ours. But what I mean is, that he's *mine*. Nothing else has ever felt like mine before, nothing like this. He belongs to us—we created him. I don't think I have or will ever love anything as much as him ever again."

Patrick felt like his heart would burst; pride and love had consumed him. Jodie had been amazing during Lewis's birth, and he was so incredibly proud of her for bringing him into the world safely. He owed his life to her for giving him the best gift that you could ever possibly give.

"Unless we have more, that is?"

Jodie laughed gently. "Let's give this little one time to settle first before we create a football team."

Patrick stood up and moved across to the window in the hospital ward. It was stifling hot outside, and the hospital staff didn't allow fans to be brought in, in case of spread of infection.

There were three other beds on Jodie's ward, all of which were unoccupied, which he found strange. They were going home the next morning, and Jodie couldn't wait to get Lewis settled into his new home. "I can't wait to be home and be a family with you both."

Patrick turned from the window and smiled widely as Jodie placed Lewis into the cot and covered him with a blanket. He drank in the fact he was a dad, wholly responsible for the tiny person he'd helped to create. He couldn't be happier and beamed at how much he loved Lewis and Jodie right at that moment. He took in the perfect picture of his wife and his son sitting by the bed and understood he would have to make sacrifices for both of them for the rest of his life.

"Do you fancy a tea?" he asked Jodie.

"That would be nice."

Patrick kissed Lewis on the head as he slept and made his way down to the café in the Queen Elizabeth University Hospital. He took his time, walking slower than he normally would, considering his new responsibility and what it would mean for the career side of his life. Being a psychic medium had its rewards, but it also meant meddling in another being that had proved dangerous for him and Jodie in the past. Of course, that would never happen again but he wasn't sure that he ever wanted to take that risk. The risk was even higher now Lewis had arrived, and Patrick never wanted to put him in any kind of danger because he could speak to the dead. Lewis wouldn't even be here if Ross Turner had succeeded in his plan. Fortunately, Patrick had been one step ahead.

Patrick found himself in front of the tea and coffee machine and pressed for two teas after sliding the coins into the slot.

Walking back to the ward, he heard Lewis crying. His heart swelled at the sound of his son's heartbreak. He entered the ward and found Jodie rocking him gently as she stood by the window. She looked up as she saw Patrick. "Wind."

"Is he okay?"

"He will be. Just need to rub his back, and he'll be fine."

Patrick placed the tea on the bedside stand and went to Jodie's side. He held his arms out. "Can I?"

Jodie handed Lewis over, who was grumbling in the process. He was tiny in Patrick's arms, and Jodie felt tears sting her eyes. Lewis grumbled a little more and then settled in his dad's arms.

"Seems okay now," Patrick said, gently swaying Lewis back and forth.

"You're a pro." Jodie wiped a tear from her eye.

"Go to sleep, Jodie. You'll be home this time tomorrow, and everything will be perfect." He looked up, expecting a protest, but she was already asleep.

"Well, little man, you've only been in the world eight hours and already you're tiring out your poor mum."

Patrick sat in the chair next to the bed and watched his wife and son as they slept peacefully. He knew then he had to consider the possibility of giving up his place in the world of mediums. It wouldn't be easy, but if it meant a better life for his family, then that's what would have to happen. There would be a lot to do— he would have to find someone to take over the church and find a full-time job to pay for the house. But he didn't care what it took, as long as Jodie and Lewis were always happy and safe.

"You sure you really want to do that?" he heard Jodie ask.

Patrick smiled. "You're not supposed to listen to my private thoughts."

"They're only private if they don't involve me and our son." Her eyes were still closed.

"It's the best thing for all of us."

Jodie nodded gently. "I know. It's been such a big part of our lives for so long. You're sure you really want to throw it away?"

"I'm not throwing it away. I'm going to find someone to take over. Obviously, I will still run it until the right person comes along. I need to give it up for us, for Lewis. I can't live for the dead anymore, Jodie."

21

"I think I'll have the omelette with a side order of vegetables," Deborah said after scanning the menu. "What about you?"

"Probably the fish," Sam replied.

The sun shone brightly through the window, and it warmed their skin. Deborah had been blissfully happy in her relationship with Sam since Jenny's weird episodes had calmed down. Sam had been attentive, loving, and everything else you could imagine to make their relationship as perfect as she had always wanted.

However, strange incidents had continued happening in the flat, and they were distracting not only Deborah but Sam too. Keys jingling quietly as they hung on the key hook, the kettle switching on by itself, and walking out of a room one minute and the next walking back in to find all of the windows open as wide as they could go.

Sam was always reassuring, though, and would laugh off the events. Deborah wasn't stupid—she knew what was going on scared them all, but she preferred to go along with Sam's uncaring attitude. She knew his attitude towards the situation wouldn't last.

The waitress approached the table. Without looking up from her little pad of paper, she said, "What can I get for you?"

"Claire," Sam greeted her.

The waitress glanced up from her pad and beamed a smile at him. "How've you been?"

Deborah's stomach lurched as she watched her man engage in conversation with another female. This female was pretty, with short dark hair and rosy cheeks; this was not good. Deborah cleared her throat to distract Sam.

"Oh, Deborah, this is Claire. She has been a waitress here for a long time. You've actually met before, on one of our first dates." Sam beamed.

Claire smiled at Deborah. "Hi."

Deborah returned the smile; however, it barely lifted the corners of her mouth. "I'm sorry, but I'm having trouble placing you."

Claire pursed her lips but didn't reply.

Sam turned from Deborah to face Claire again. "She'll have the omelette and a side order of vegetables, and I'll have my usual."

Usual? Deborah suddenly thought. *How often is he in here without me?*

Claire scribbled the order down. "I'll have it with you shortly."

Deborah watched as Claire walked back to the kitchen and disappeared behind the door. She turned to Sam, not wanting to spoil the afternoon. "She seems nice."

Sam nodded, unaware Deborah was gritting her teeth and wringing her hands together. "Yeah, she's worked here for ages. Just know her from coming in all the time."

"With Jenny?"

"Not always. Sometimes come in for a takeaway before work, especially if I'm rehearsing. She always throws in an extra sausage or toast."

Deborah smiled through her anger and knew the best thing to do would be to change the subject and steer Sam from wanting to come back to this café again, from wanting to see Claire. "What do you want to do tonight?" she asked.

"Sorry, babe, got rehearsals at the theatre tonight. Will probably be out to well after midnight. The show is less than a month away, so it'll be all go for the next month."

Deborah grinned. "If you have to work, then you have to work. I'll wait up for you. Maybe there'll be a surprise on your arrival."

Sam returned the grin. "I'll make sure I get my lines perfect, in that case."

Claire returned with their food, and Deborah found it best not to look at her. After their meal, Deborah excused herself from the table, and she made her way to the bathroom. She sat down on the seat and tried to rid herself of the jealousy that had taken over her mind. She knew Sam loved her, and he would never cheat on her, but there was something in Claire she didn't like. Perhaps the fact she was pretty, and Sam engaged in pleasant conversation was a factor, also knowing Sam had a usual meal choice, and she wasn't always with him when he was in the café.

Deborah's thoughts were interrupted by two women entering the bathroom. They were giggling, and she recognised Claire's voice straight away.

"He gets better looking every time I see him," she heard Claire say.

"I know, he's flawless: that jawline, his hair. He looks even better in real life than he does on telly," girl number two replied.

"If he were single, I would definitely ask him out."

Deborah smiled as she opened the cubicle door. She met Claire's eyes in the mirror, and Claire's rosy cheeks drained away.

"Uh…" was all Claire could say.

"You're right, he's better looking in real life. And you know what else?" Deborah spoke as she casually washed her hands.

Girl number two didn't know where to look. "We're just messing about."

Deborah ignored her. "He's fantastic in bed too. And he's all mine, so if you were planning on waiting until he's single, you'll be waiting a very long time." She stuck her hands under the hand dryer, and even though her heart wanted to burst out of her chest, she kept her composure.

"Look, there's no harm here. It's a bit of girly banter," Claire said.

Deborah turned to face her, and as the hand dryer switched itself off, the silence which filled the room was chilling. She didn't reply to Claire's words; she simply walked through the girls and left the bathroom. She lingered for a moment, listening to what Claire had to say for herself after the subtle confrontation.

"Jesus, she's a bloody head case!"

"That's nothing; you should meet his friend Jenny. I don't know what it is he does to women, but after that, I don't think he will be back in here, not without *her* anyhow."

"You think they're a threesome?"

Claire laughed. "No. I don't know, but whatever the relationship is between those three, it's weird. The funny thing is, he seems oblivious to it."

Deborah walked away from the opposite side of the door when she heard the flush of a toilet.

Sam looked up as she reached the table. "You ready?"

Deborah nodded as she picked up her coat and followed Sam out to the street. "Ready as I'll ever be."

22

Jodie was happy she had settled Lewis into their home at Henderson Manor. She had mentioned to Patrick about perhaps changing the name on the plaque at the front of the house from Henderson Manor simply to McLaughlin. The name Henderson Manor did not suit the modern-day reality the house was now a part of. It almost sounded more like a horror was being filmed on the grounds, rather than a new family building a life there. Patrick hadn't understood the urgency in her suggestion and thought there were more important things they should be thinking about rather than the name of their house.

"I just don't like it. When Lewis is at school, the kids will make fun of him," she had stressed.

"You think the kids at his school won't like him because his house has a name? Come on, Jodie. Don't be ridiculous."

She knew it sounded unreasonable, but something inside her didn't feel right. Henderson Manor sounded like the setting of some old legendary horror tale. "I'm not being ridiculous; I'm saying I want to change it. And anyway, we're not called Henderson, we're McLaughlin, so if anything, it should be called McLaughlin Manor or McLaughlin House."

Patrick nodded. "We can call it that, if it means that much to you. We'll change the plaque, too, but not now. We have to decorate this place, and if you haven't already noticed, it's going to be a big job."

The conversation was left at that, and Jodie didn't mention it again. She wanted to focus on how to be a good mum to Lewis, and for their new family to work, she thought it best to forget about renaming the house. It was a little ridiculous how strongly she felt about it, and she couldn't quite put her finger on why. Jodie put it down to the fact she wanted the house to be in their name and not some other family who had no living relatives left.

"I'm not speaking or thinking ill of the dead, you'll understand," Jodie had said aloud as she watered the flowers next to the memorials at the back of the house. "I want this to be *our* home. Time moves on, and things change; we won't completely erase you from the house. We couldn't, even if we wanted to. There's too much history here; a coat of paint and a roll of wallpaper couldn't erase that."

Since Patrick had told Jodie about the connection which he had made to one of the deceased Henderson family members before Lewis was born, nothing else had happened, which Jodie was glad of. Whatever meaning was behind the message had obviously not meant enough for them to carry on contacting Patrick.

Jodie looked up when she heard Lewis babbling from his pram. She had moved the seat upwards and pulled the hood up to shield his little head from the sun. Even though it wasn't hot, she didn't want to risk him burning. His little eyes darted back and forth, taking in the bright colours and sounds around him. He spotted his mum as she approached the pram, and his little legs bounced up and down. His pink, toothless smile melted Jodie each time she looked at him.

"Hi, baby. Are you laughing at Mummy talking to herself?" she asked softly as she lifted Lewis from the pram.

At eight months old, he smiled constantly which reminded Jodie each day why she had decided to give up her place at the church. Spending every day with her son had made her realise life was much more than death. With the greatest of respect for the dead, Jodie knew her heart no longer lay with them, and all she wanted was to be a mum and a wife.

"Come on, baby boy. Let's get you to the park and see if we can feed those ducks."

Walking with Lewis had become a daily occurrence, and she had managed to get back to her pre-pregnancy weight. Jodie enjoyed walking around the park with Lewis, listening to him babble to himself and coo as the gentle breeze touched his face. She would never have thought a baby's voice could be so tranquil.

As she reached the park bench she sat on each day, she put on the back brake of the pram, made sure Lewis was covered with his blanket as he slept and took out her book. The weather was pleasantly warm for late February, and the breeze had faded, so Jodie felt comfortable to sit there for as long as she could.

Feeling content Lewis would have his full two-hour afternoon nap, Jodie opened her book and lost herself within the pages of a story far from the world she knew to be reality.

"Hello," came an unfamiliar voice which startled her.

Jodie looked up and saw a young woman sitting beside her on the bench. Lewis was still fast asleep, cosy under his blanket.

"Hi," was all Jodie could manage. It was all she wanted to manage; whoever this person was, she had interrupted the peacefulness of reading and escaping from the world for just a few hours. She lowered her head back into the book and scanned the page, looking for the words her eyes last read.

"Is this your son?" The woman asked again.

No, I stole him from the hospital! Jodie thought sarcastically but knew better and answered more politely, "Yes, he is."

She didn't feel comfortable with how close the woman was and discreetly shuffled along the bench by leaning into the pram's basket underneath to check her mobile phone, even though she knew it was switched off.

The woman stayed in the same place on the bench and continued to look at Lewis as he slept.

"Can I help you with something?" Jodie said, hiding the irritation in her voice.

The woman smiled. "Sorry, I like to sit here sometimes. I hope you don't mind."

Jodie shook her head. "I don't mind. I sit here every day at this time, but I've never come across you."

The woman smiled again and looked across the duck pond ahead of them. "My mum used to bring me here when I was a baby. She told me when I slept in the pram, she would sit and read, like you are now."

Just like I was, until you interrupted me, Jodie thought. And then, she instantly felt guilty. She could tell this woman was reminiscing about her mum, who was obviously no longer with her. She had spoken to enough people in the church over the years to understand when someone spoke fondly of a past loved one.

"Are you okay?" Jodie found herself asking.

"It reminded me of my mum telling me that when I saw you. It was nice to see this bench is still being used for that purpose."

Jodie felt this woman's heart aching, but she sensed it wasn't just for her dead mother.

"I'm Jodie," she said, with a smile.

"Nice to meet you, Jodie. And who is this little chap?" the woman asked as she peered into the pram.

"This is Lewis. He's my first."

The woman looked at Jodie and said nothing. Instead, she stared into her eyes, as if searching for something.

"What?" Jodie asked. She frowned at the woman, not knowing how to take her.

The woman's eyes were suddenly dark, and shadows fell over her face. "You're living in a house you no longer feel comfortable with. You don't know why you suddenly feel this way, but you'll soon find out, and when you do, you'll want to get out of there and stay away. Bad things will happen in that house; you don't want your little Lewis to experience any of it."

Jodie was stunned by the woman's sudden outburst of words. "Hang on a minute. How do you know about my house?"

"Let's say I knew the family who once lived there." The woman stood up, smiled down at Lewis, and then cast her eyes upon Jodie once more. "Think about what I've said. Something will come into your life you have been trying to keep out since you found out you were going to have your baby, and you won't be able to stop it."

***

Lewis cried loudly, and Jodie opened her eyes. She had fallen asleep on the bench, and her book was on her lap at the page she had opened it at. She picked Lewis out of his pram and noticed on her watch that he had had his two-hour nap, which meant she had had a two-hour nap.

"Jesus," she whispered to herself. "How could I have fallen asleep in the bloody park?"

She put Lewis back in the pram and covered him again with the blanket. As she made her way toward the gate which led to the street, she silently cursed herself. *How the hell could I be so bloody stupid? Anyone could have taken him!*

As she passed the last bench of the park before the gate, she saw a woman sitting there. The dream flashed into her mind, and she remembered that the woman in her dream was the woman sitting on the bench.

As Jodie passed through the gate, the woman smiled at her and waved to little Lewis as he chewed on his fingers. Jodie walked quicker.

Lewis giggled as the woman waved to him until he and Jodie were no longer in her line of sight.

23

"See you in the morning!" Claire called out as she left the café. Every Friday, the café had a late license where customers could bring a bottle of wine and have a meal. The only thing was it was open until midnight, and somehow, Claire always ended up on the early shift the next morning.

The air had grown chilly, and she wrapped her coat around her tightly as she walked along the street to the flat she shared with her mum. Claire turned up the side street at Kelvin Hall, and knowing her mum would kill her if she knew she had taken that route, Claire increased her speed to get home.

The breeze caused the bare trees to sway, creating a low hush in the air which harmonized with the rush of the canal below. The lights along the street which housed the old Transport Museum were dimly lit, and the stars twinkled above her. Halfway along the street, she became lost in her thoughts about what life would be like had she completed her university course. She would've been able to get her mum away from Glasgow, and the memories that tempted her lips back to the bottle. Claire knew her mum was getting better as the years went on, and that the flower shop was doing well. It kept her busy and her mind off the booze, but she couldn't help worry it would always be part of her. Claire knew there was nothing she could ever do to change the way her mum was, but she would do everything she could to keep her busy. That was why she decided to help her develop her hobby of gardening and develop it into a business.

After Claire's dad had died from cancer ten years previously, she watched as her mum spiralled into depression which drove her to drink. It started out as a few glasses of wine at night, then it quickly progressed to a bottle, then two, and before Claire knew it, her mum was drinking a litre of vodka every two days. The drink almost killed her, and the only thing that stopped it from happening was the thought Claire would be left on her own without any parents. Claire was strong for both of them, and as her mum got better, she went out to work and kept the household running.

This had brought them closer together, and Claire not only had a mum but a best friend and a sister. That was why Claire was always worrying but would never let it be known.

The flower shop was what kept her mum going during the day, and at night, Claire would cook, and they would have a meal together, except, of course, for a Friday when Claire worked late.

Claire had become so lost in her thoughts she hadn't noticed she was being followed. The figure behind her kept a safe distance and stayed within the shadows of the old Transport Museum building. Claire crossed the empty car park and heard the leaves crunching beneath her shoes. The sound merged with the sounds of the wind and the rushing of the canal so she didn't even hear the fast approaching footsteps behind her.

At first, she thought she was being mugged and so held onto her bag as tightly as she could. However, it wasn't until she saw the glint of the blade sparkle under the moonlight that she knew this was more than a mugging.

She let go of her bag and tried to run, but the person in black grabbed at her hair and pulled her back. Claire tried to scream, but the sound wouldn't come as the shock took over. The pain in her neck came in waves and seemed to spread over her whole body. She put her hand up to protect herself and felt her neck was wet.

On observing her hand, even in the darkness she knew the wetness was blood and lots of it.

The person who had stabbed her was gone. She hadn't noticed the person leave, and she hadn't cared; she just wanted to get home. Her legs would no longer carry her, and she collapsed to the cold ground with the gravel crunching under her weight.

Claire looked up at the building where she shared the flat with her mum and could see the kitchen light was on; she was *that* close to home.

Suddenly, she found she couldn't breathe, and everything was happening in slow motion. She reached for the bag she had ditched in the hope she could phone an ambulance, but she couldn't move her body.

A car passed by on Old Dumbarton Road, heading towards the children's hospital, but with the car park in almost complete darkness, no one saw Claire was sprawled on the ground, taking her last breath.

There was nothing Claire could do but hope it would be over quickly. She had always been afraid of an early death from her experience with her dad; however, she found peace in the fact if there was a heaven, then she might get to see him again.

Her eyes filled with tears at the realisation she was about to die on her own, on the ground of a car park outside her home, and there was no one around to help her. She closed her eyes to allow the tears to fall.

She never opened them again.

24

Walking along the road in the rain at six o'clock in the morning with an excitable dog on the end of the lead was not his idea of fun, but fifteen-year old Gregory had no choice. His mother had told him if he wanted to go on the family holiday, he had to find a way of earning some spending money or it wasn't going to happen. So, he had offered to be the one to walk the family dog, every day. He hadn't believed his mum and dad would actually make him keep his word, but he was wrong.

With the cold wintery weather truly making its presence known, Gregory couldn't help but imagine walking along the beach in Lanzarote and feeling the hot sand beneath his feet. The cool water lapping around his toes and the sound of the gentle Canary Island breeze whirling around him was enough to accept walking Dennis, the hyperactive Labrador puppy. At six months old, the thing was close to fully grown, and he was almost pulling Gregory off his feet.

"Wait!" Gregory said in a firm voice.

The dog ignored his command and continued panting his way up the street. Gregory's images of Lanzarote were blown from his mind as the wind picked up, causing a strong gust to lift the crisp packets which littered the street and create a cyclone of colourful foil.

"This is just great for a Saturday morning," he said to himself.

Gregory was doubtful the sun would shine today, what with the rain and wind during the night. The weather had been reasonable when he had gone to bed, but it had woken him in the middle of the night with the rain lashing off the window.

His immediate thought was that his alarm clock would be going off in a few hours and the knowledge of taking Dennis for a walk was not what he had in mind for his Saturday morning. But it would only be for twenty minutes, and then, he could take Dennis home and climb back into bed. That was, if Dennis didn't drag him home instead; the damn dog was so strong and full of energy all of the time.

"Slow down, you stupid mutt," Gregory said as Dennis almost strangled himself trying to pull them along the street.

They turned down Bunhouse Street, away from the main road into the city centre and the old museum building sheltered them slightly from the wind. Dennis stopped suddenly and barked once. Gregory took no notice as he continued to walk. However, Dennis continued to bark furiously, and his tail whipped from side to side. Gregory looked down at the dog as he continued to bark and wag his tail. Dennis never barked unless the door went or they were about to go out.

"What is it, boy?"

Gregory allowed Dennis to lead him towards the car park, and by the looks of it, Dennis knew where he wanted to go. Bunhouse Street car park was empty, and there was nobody else around. The trees cast large shadows across the car park, and the street lights twinkled behind the branches blowing in the wind. Before Gregory knew it, he was standing by himself, and he had let go of Dennis's lead. He watched as Dennis sniffed around the bulk on the ground, and his tail had stopped wagging.

"What have you found, boy?" Gregory called.

Dennis barked again, allowing Gregory's suspicions to grow. He knew it was likely to be what he expected, but he didn't want it to be. He approached the dog slowly, and on his approach, the dog would normally become excited, but not now. He reached the bulky heap and looked down; what his eyes saw were not what a fifteen-year-old boy should have to see. There was a lot of blood along the jawline and the upper part of the body. The gash in the neck was neat, where he presumed a knife would have made its entrance.

Gregory was frozen in fear, not sure what he should do. He jumped as his mobile phone rang in his pocket. His hands scrambled to find the device.

"Hello?"

"Gregory, if there is a shop open, grab some milk." His mum's voice was on the other end of the phone.

"Mum?" his voice shook.

There was a silent pause.

"You've lost the dog again, haven't you?" she whined.

Gregory shook his head slowly. "I've found something."

"What?"

Gregory swung his body away from the bloodied corpse as he retched. He held the phone away from his face, but could hear his mum's panicked words through the speaker. Putting the phone to his ear, he spoke. "I'm at the old museum. Come quick. I've found a body."

25

Lang held up his badge to the uniformed officer guarding the forensics tent, and he lifted the material to allow him and Preston inside.

"Yet another Glasgow murder." Preston sighed as they looked down at the woman on the ground.

The flash of the camera reflected the bright white material of the tent, and Lang could feel another headache threatening. He massaged his temples as he took in the scene. "What do you think? Unprovoked?"

Preston nodded. "Possibly. A jealous boyfriend, perhaps?"

"Could be a number of things at this stage. We'll need to ask the next of kin as much as we can to determine the company the girl keeps…"

"Kept," Preston corrected.

"Aye, we'll need to find out where she worked, who she worked with, if she had any—what is it the kids say these days?—beef with anyone?"

Preston smiled. "Why are you doing that? Act your age, man."

Lang beckoned the forensic officer in charge. "Do we have an identity on the girl yet?"

The forensic officer nodded. "Yes. According to her student card, her name is Claire Prowse. She was twenty-three, and her address is forty-four Ferry Road, which, if I'm not mistaken, is just down there." He pointed in the direction of the flats at the bottom of the main road.

"Jesus, she was on her way home." Preston shook his head.

Lang narrowed his eyes as they exited the tent. "We'll wait until they've moved the body before we inform the next of kin.

We don't want them seeing this and knowing it's their daughter or whatever."

Preston and Lang went back to the car, and all the while, Lang still was massaging his temples.

"You okay there, Jim?"

"Eh?" Lang looked up. "Aye, got a headache."

"Another one? That's the fourth this week. You'd better get to the doctor and get that seen to."

Lang nodded. "I will. But we've been too busy for me to get away."

Preston climbed into the car, shaking his head as he did so. "Always excuses with you."

"Who are you, my mother?"

"I'm just saying if you've got a constant headache, maybe you need glasses."

"Then I'll go to the bloody optician."

There was silence. Lang had been snappy for weeks, and Preston was getting a little sick of it.

"Do you know what? Next time, I won't bloody bother."

Lang put his seat belt on and was glad Preston had shut up. There was enough going on with Preston's imminent retirement and a new murder enquiry. He didn't have the want or the time to be going to the doctor.

"Let's go and wait for the call the body has been moved so we can inform next of kin and try to piece together her last movements."

***

Linda Prowse dialled her daughter's number for the millionth time that morning, but she still couldn't get past the voicemail. It wasn't like Claire to stay out all night and not tell her mum where she was. Something definitely wasn't right. Linda punched the local police station's number into the keypad.

"I'd like to report my daughter missing."

Linda explained the situation to the officer at the end of the phone, and before she knew it, the buzzer in the flat was sounding.

On opening the door, she instantly recognised the men. "You're the two officers who I spoke to when Zoe Henderson died."

Preston smiled, unaware of how to answer that, considering what they were about to tell her. "Can we come in, Mrs Prowse?"

Linda opened the door wider and welcomed them in. "You see, my daughter, Claire, she didn't come home from work last night, and if she had planned on staying out, she would have told me, and she hasn't. I can't get her on her mobile, and well, I just panicked. All I could think to do was to report her missing."

"Mrs Prowse, we actually have some news about your daughter." Lang hated this part of the job. He was glad he didn't have to do it too often. Usually, it would be uniform who would take this responsibility, but seeing as they already had knowledge of Claire Prowse's demise, they saw it as the best thing to do to be the ones to deliver the news.

"Oh God, what is it?" Linda Prowse wrung her hands together, eyes glistening with threatening tears.

Preston took a deep breath before he began. "A body was found in Bunhouse Street car park at six o'clock this morning. We believe the identity to be Claire. I'm sorry, Mrs Prowse."

Linda Prowse fell back onto the couch. "I want to see her."

Lang nodded. "Of course. We can arrange for that today."

Preston sat down beside her. "Is there anyone you can call?"

Linda Prowse shook her head. "It was just the two of us."

Lang turned to face the door, disgusted that, yet again, they had had to tell some poor woman her daughter had been murdered. Professionalism took over, and he turned to face Linda once more. "I'll make the call and arrange for an official identification, Mrs Prowse."

Linda didn't take any notice. She turned to Preston, who was trying to stop himself from imagining what it would be like if it were one of his two beautiful girls. "What happened to her?"

"Mrs Prowse, Claire has a stab wound to the neck. She was murdered."

Linda Prowse stared through Preston, like he wasn't there.

Silence filled the room, and Preston stood up as Lang entered the room. "We can take you now, Mrs Prowse. Are you sure you want to do this so soon?"

Linda Prowse was already on her feet. "Yes, I want to see her. I need to…to believe it's her."

Denial was evidently sailing through Linda's mind as she followed Lang and Preston out to their car. Her face failed her attempts at bravery, and Preston was sure she would cave at any moment. She didn't say anything as they made the journey to Glasgow City Morgue.

***

On arrival, Preston and Lang led Linda Prowse down a long, white corridor which smelled of death and decay. Of course, the place was clean, but Linda could smell nothing other than death masked with bleach. It turned her stomach to think her daughter may be lying on a cold concrete slab somewhere in that building.

"What do I have to do?" Linda asked suddenly, her voice cracking.

"We'll sit outside and wait to be called in. You will go into the room; one of us can accompany you, if you'd like. All you have to do is tell us if it's Claire, and you can leave as soon as you wish afterwards." Lang found he was speaking with the softest voice he had ever used. It seemed to help his headache. The bright white walls did not.

"I'll go in by myself."

"Okay, that's fine. Take as long as you need," Lang replied.

Linda Prowse sat down on the cold plastic seat outside what, to her, looked like the doorway of an office with a mirrored window beside it.

***

An eternity passed by inside what turned out to be just a few minutes, and a pathologist invited Linda inside. Her stomach flipped. Her heartbeat echoed in her head, and she could hear the blood rushing in her ears. Everything slowed down and became blurry as she watched the pathologist lift the crisp white sheet from the head of the corpse on the concrete slab. She looked down and saw her daughter. Her face no longer smiling and full of light, but instead, shadows cast across her pale skin, and dreadful fear filled Linda. Had her daughter suffered terrible pain in her last moments? And who had put her on that slab?

"Yes. That's Claire."

Linda turned before the pathologist covered Claire's face and was out of the door and back on the plastic seat next to Preston and Lang.

"It's her. My baby girl. It's her." Linda said, with a mixture of shock and anger in her voice.

"Thank you, Mrs Prowse. I can't imagine how hard that must have been for you to do," Preston said.

Linda stood up, and the officers rose with her. "Find the bastard who murdered my daughter before I do."

26

Sam had managed to cover up his real feelings about the things that had been happening in his flat over the past year or so. Deborah and Jenny had been scared at first, but seeing Sam calm about the situation made the girls calm, and so things seemed relatively normal for them. But deep down, Sam knew these things were happening for a reason, even if he didn't want to admit it out loud. He had never really considered life after death until he experienced the things happening right under his nose. The slamming of doors, the windows opening, the kitchen appliances turning themselves on and off...how could that be explained rationally? He had managed to hide most of it from the girls, although they would occasionally witness small things, like tapping sounds and the temperature dramatically dropping.

Standing outside the main entrance to the church, he found himself clutching at the small cutting from the advert in the paper about the West End Spiritualist Church and all its offerings. Sam had never given the 'afterlife' a second thought until recent events made him question what was really going on in his and Jenny's flat. All he knew was he was standing outside the church, ready to go inside and try to figure out what was going on.

"You okay there, son?"

Sam turned to find a little old lady looking up at him and smiling kindly. She was half Sam's size and was clutching at her handbag.

"Yes, I'm fine, thank you. Is this the West End Spiritualist Church?" Sam already knew it was; he didn't know why he was asking.

"Aye, it is, son. This here is the best place to come if you're looking for comfort after the death of a loved one, or if you're looking to find peace. Is that why you're here?" Her voice was soft but with a broad Glaswegian twang behind it.

"You could say that." Sam returned the smile.

He followed the old lady inside and found there was already a building audience. Sam didn't know entirely what he was going to say, if he were going to say anything at all. He felt slightly ridiculous he had come to someone who claimed to speak to the dead about some bumps in the night in his flat. However, he had no other ideas and had hoped this medium could shed some light on the subject.

"It's your first time, is it?" the old lady asked as she sat down beside him.

Sam nodded.

"You'll like it here; Patrick is spot on almost every time he gives a reading."

"Patrick?"

"Aye, Patrick is the medium for tonight. There are others in the city, but he and his wife, Jodie, are the best by far, although, since Jodie had the baby, she doesn't really do readings anymore. Shame, really — she was always great at making you feel better about a loved one's passing."

Sam tried to concentrate on the stage at the front of the room. For some reason, he felt terrified, and he didn't understand why.

"Don't look so scared, son. You'll be fine."

The bustle of the room distracted Sam for a little while before the demonstration began. He watched the people that poured into the room and wondered why they were here, who they were here for, and if it would make them feel better. Sam watched a man approach the stage and realised he had picked a seat in the front row.

Nice one, Sam, he thought.

The bustle of the room lessened until there was silence, and everyone turned their eyes to the man who was standing two feet above them on the small stage.

"Good evening, everyone, and thank you all for attending tonight's demonstration. As many of you are already aware, my name is Patrick McLaughlin, and I'm the head medium at this church. Are there any newcomers in the audience this evening?"

Sam reluctantly raised his hand, wishing he had sat at the back to get a look at who else was new.

"A few tonight. I will welcome you all and give you my quick spiel before I move onto the readings. My aim is to provide you with as accurate a reading as possible from whoever may come to me tonight. If I come to you and offer you information, all I need for you to do is say, yes, if you understand, or no, if you don't."

Sam felt his palms sweat. *Why am I so bloody nervous?*

"I don't aim to scare, upset or give anyone negative information during the readings, and so if you feel any of these things, I need you to tell me you do not wish to continue, and I will move onto someone else."

The little old lady nudged Sam, and when he turned to her, she winked at him. "That never happens. He's always fantastic," she whispered.

"Let's begin."

Patrick fell silent along with the audience, and his eyes scanned the room. A few moments passed, and he nodded a few times, as if agreeing with something. Sam almost got up and left, but froze in his seat when Patrick's eyes fell on his.

"Sam?"

Sam's eyes widened, and his throat almost seized up. He nodded.

"You've come here for help this evening."

Patrick moved along the stage slowly, back and forth, saying nothing for a few moments.

"It seems you have had a visitor, and you wish for them to leave?" Patrick enhanced the last word to make it sound like a question, even though he and Sam both knew it was not a question but a confirmation.

"Yes, that's correct; I think."

Patrick nodded. "I do not wish to continue this reading in the public gallery. We will meet at the end of my demonstrations tonight, if that's okay with you."

Sam was shocked, and before he knew it, Patrick had moved onto someone else entirely.

What the hell does he know?

***

Patrick closed the door of the church when the last person left and turned to face Sam. He was surprised Sam had stayed at all; he had fully expected to see him leave as soon as he had said they would speak after the demonstration.

"So, you have something to say that can't be said in front of an audience?" Sam asked. It sounded like an interrogation, although it wasn't meant that way.

"I didn't say it *couldn't* be said in front of the audience. I just thought out of courtesy for you it would be better if we spoke in private."

"And I suppose you'll charge me a fee for that?" Sam asked.

Patrick shook his head. "No, I offered for you to stay."

Sam nodded in defeat. He had expected to have to pay an up-front fee before any words were exchanged. Patrick led Sam to a small room in another part of the building and offered for him to sit down.

"So, you seem to have a lot on your mind," Patrick said.

"You know?"

"I have been made aware of your visitor."

"Visitor?"

"The bumps in the night, the photo frames falling off the walls, the items going missing and turning up somewhere else?"

Sam couldn't help but smile. "You think I have a ghost?"

Patrick returned the smile which slowly turned to a grin. "Why else would you be here?"

Sam couldn't believe what he was hearing. Thinking of it, he couldn't believe he was considering it to be a possibility. "No way. Ghosts don't exist. This is ridiculous."

Patrick nodded. "So, why are you here, then?"

Sam couldn't reply. He didn't know why he had come to the church. "Desperation, I suppose."

Patrick sighed. "I'm not one to force my ability on anyone, so if you're not sure you believe in what I do, then you're free to leave. I'm not going to waste your time, and I certainly don't want to waste my own."

Patrick left the small room and made his way into the main hall. He began stacking chairs and was shocked to see Sam was helping.

"I didn't say I don't believe in what you do. I'm just saying I'm not sure what to believe."

Sam had thought of multiple ways to explain what had been going on in his and Jenny's flat. But nothing seemed reasonable, not when he had seen things with his own eyes on more than one occasion. Yes, photo frames fall down all of the time, loose hooks or bad hanging to blame for that. But how do you explain the frames not just falling down but flying across the room?

"If you want my help, I'll gladly oblige. However, if you don't, then I wouldn't be offended. Many people have come here before out of sheer curiosity and found it's not their thing. But you've come here for a specific reason, am I right?"

Sam cleared his throat as he stacked the last chair. "Yes, there's a specific reason, but in my head, it's not logical."

Patrick was not surprised to hear that. "It never is logical in my line of work. If you really do want me to help you, then you have to let me help you. If not, then that's fine. Good luck with sorting it out."

"How much do I pay?" Sam asked.

Patrick laughed. "I'm not going to charge you anything. It's only a few moments of my time to find out what's going on."

Sam shook his head. "I don't know if it will be just a few moments."

"What do you mean?"

"Whatever is in my flat has steadily got worse as time has gone on."

Patrick frowned. "For me to really understand it, I'm going to have to come to your house."

27

As the bulb flickered for the umpteenth time that evening, Jenny decided to go out. She was not at all one for believing in ghost stories, however being in the flat alone when the bulbs in most of the rooms were flickering and doors were seemingly closing on their own made her skin prickle. She made her way through to her bedroom to collect her handbag when a sound from the kitchen stopped her. Being frozen with fear prevented her from going to the kitchen to investigate, and so, instead of turning around, she kept moving toward her bedroom door.

Jenny.

Not only did she hear it but she felt it to. An ice-cold breeze on the back of her neck, and she swung to where she had heard it. Nothing or no one stood behind her, but she knew something was not right. Jenny wanted to call out, but what good would it do? If she got a reply, she would probably die from a heart attack, and if she didn't get a reply, then she would probably die from fear of waiting for one. Instead, she decided to grab her handbag and leave as quickly as she could. Jenny rushed into her bedroom and hooked her arm through the straps. She then reached for her coat and didn't dare look in the mirror. Wrapping her hand around the handle of her bedroom door, she stopped.

"I didn't close the door," she whispered.

A gentle rush of air brushed the side of her face, and her body convulsed with fear. Jenny grabbed the handle and pulled the door open. Stood on the other side of the door was Sam, and she screamed.

"What?" Sam jumped back.

Jenny dropped her bag and coat and slumped down onto the bed, covering her face with her hands.

"Are you trying to send me to an early grave?"

"What is it?" Sam asked as he entered the room.

Jenny looked up. Her hands were shaking so much she had to place them on the bed at either side of her to keep them steady.

"It happened again." Jenny stopped talking when she saw another man come into her view. "Who's this?"

Sam looked behind him and saw Patrick standing in the doorway. "Oh, this is Patrick McLaughlin."

Jenny smiled gently, looking for more information.

"He's a medium."

"A medium?"

Patrick entered the room and held out his hand. "Nice to meet you; you must be Jenny?"

Jenny shook Patrick's hand and tried to control the involuntary jittery movements.

"Are you okay, Jenny?" Patrick asked.

Jenny shook her head.

"I gather from you being here, Sam has told you what has been going on?"

"He mentioned a few things."

Sam interrupted, "I told Patrick that I wasn't sure how to explain things, so he offered to come and have a look around."

Jenny stood up from the bed. "For what price? Surely your kind doesn't come cheap?"

Patrick smiled. "Actually, this is not usually in my job description. So, I'm not charging anything."

"What were you so frightened of when we first came in?" Sam asked.

Jenny told him about hearing her name and the bang from the kitchen. Patrick listened as he took in his new surroundings. Something definitely didn't feel right. There was a heavy presence in the flat, and it wasn't a happy one.

"Can I have a look around?" Patrick asked.

"Of course. It's not a big flat, so you can't get lost," Sam replied.

Patrick disappeared from their sight, and Jenny fell into Sam's arms.

"You looked terrified when you opened the door," he soothed.

"I was. I am. What the hell's going on in here?"

Sam shook his head. "I have no idea."

Jenny pulled away and ran her hands through her hair, not knowing what to do or where Patrick's visit would lead them. "Should we go with him?" Jenny asked.

The pair left Jenny's room and went into the kitchen where they found Patrick, who was standing by the breakfast bar and staring out of the window.

"Anything?" Sam asked.

"Has this been happening the whole time you've lived in this flat?" Patrick replied.

Jenny shook her head. "No, only in the last year or so. It has become progressively worse, though, and it's scaring the shit out of me."

Patrick nodded as he gazed around the kitchen. "Okay. And how long have you lived here?"

"About two and a half years," Sam replied. "These flats have been up for about three. And I own this one."

"Why do you ask?" Jenny prompted.

"Just trying to establish all the facts."

Patrick left the kitchen and made his way into the living area. He stopped suddenly, and Sam almost walked into the back of him.

"What is it?" Sam asked warily.

"Who's Zoe?"

Jenny gasped at the sound of her name.

"She's my ex. And, yes, before you ask, she's dead. And, no, I didn't kill her."

Sam's attempts at comedy failed him miserably when neither Patrick nor Jenny even cracked a smile.

"Why do you mention Zoe?" Jenny asked.

Patrick turned to face them both. "Your relationship with her didn't end well, did it?"

Sam's head ached. This can't be happening. He knew what Patrick was about to say next, and suddenly wished he hadn't gone to the church at all. He would rather not know.

"No, it didn't end well. But there were many reasons for that, and the police have proven they were factual."

"Police?" Patrick asked.

Sam nodded, and Jenny sat down on the sofa.

"Zoe kind of lost the plot when we were together, hated that I was living with Jenny. She became jealous, so jealous she sent hate mail to Jenny. And I would receive photographs of Zoe and me together and Jenny and me together. On the back of them, she'd written, *he's mine* and *she's dead.* She did a lot of really sick stuff and tried to make it look like someone was stalking me when it turned out to be her all along."

Patrick frowned. "How did you know it was she who was sending you those things?"

"When she died, the police turned up asking me questions about her and how things were between us the last time I had seen her. Anyway, they found a bunch of photos, letters, and other stuff in a box in Zoe's house. They confirmed to me it was most likely she who was stalking us." Sam stopped talking for a few moments. "I didn't want to have to go through all of this again."

"I'm sorry. But if you want me to help you, I have to know everything."

Jenny sniggered. "If you're so psychic, then how come you don't know it all already?"

Patrick didn't retaliate. He smiled gently and considered his answer before he spoke. "Because, Jenny, I'm not a mind reader. I'm a spiritualist medium, and I don't always have the full background."

Jenny opened her mouth to reply, when music began playing. It was coming from the other end of the flat, and it was getting louder by the second.

Sam raced through towards the music to find it was coming from his bedroom. It wasn't that music had begun randomly playing that was giving him chills but the song: Elvis Presley, 'The Wonder of You.'

"No way," was all that Sam could say.

Patrick turned the music off and turned to Sam. "She used to sing it all the time, didn't she?"

Sam's face was drained of colour. What was normally a fresh rosy face was now the look of death.

"*All* the time."

Sam didn't want to believe it. However, he knew what Patrick was about to say next.

"Sam?" Jenny placed her hand on his shoulder.

Patrick looked at the terrified faces of the people standing in front of him and knew that they understood. "When Zoe died, I don't think she went very far. I think she's here, in this flat."

Jenny shuddered. "Oh my god, this is ridiculous." Her faked confidence failed her; she couldn't hide the fear in her voice.

"It explains a lot though, doesn't it?" Sam looked down at her. "Question is, why is this happening?"

Patrick hadn't anticipated this at all. "I think she has some unfinished business. But not with you."

They all jumped at the sound of Sam's mobile ringing loudly in his pocket. He took the phone in his hand and looked down at the screen.

"Excuse me please," he said as he left the bedroom and went into the hall to answer.

Jenny was left standing in Sam's room with Patrick, and she looked him straight in the eye. "Do you honestly not know who she could be here for?"

Patrick shook his head.

"Do you think it could be me?"

"I don't mean to scare you, but if what Sam said about the stalking is true, then it's a possibility."

Jenny's eyes glistened against the moonlight filtering through the window. "She hated that we were — are — best friends. She wanted him to stop being friends with me. She hated me. I could see it in her eyes. Of course, she denied everything, and I kept my mouth shut whenever Sam spoke to her about me. You think that she wants revenge?"

Patrick narrowed his eyes. "Revenge for what?"

"For not getting her own way, and for not getting her claws into Sam. For dying before she could really do some serious damage?"

"You really think Zoe was so jealous of your friendship with Sam that she would have gone on to do something far worse?"

Jenny shrugged. "Who knows? She was pretty crazy when Sam broke up with her."

Patrick rubbed the back of his neck. "How did she die?"

"The police said it was accidental. She fell down the stairs in her house, apparently. She lived by herself in a huge house that was left to her in some family will. I seriously thought Sam was set for life when he first started seeing her; clearly, he wasn't."

Patrick sat down on the bed, wondering what to do next.

"Are you all right?" Jenny asked.

Sam entered the room, still holding the phone. "That was Deborah on the phone. She's coming over."

Patrick's mind was buzzing as he tried to piece together all of the information he had received so far. But something didn't feel right. "Sam, what did you say Zoe's surname was?"

"I didn't say, but it was Henderson. Zoe Henderson. Why?"

Patrick stood up and ran his hand across his head. "Jenny said that Zoe lived in a huge house that was left to her in a family will, is that correct?"

Sam nodded.

"Okay, well, in that case, I think I've bought Zoe's house: Henderson Manor."

28

Sam felt deflated after Patrick had left, almost like someone had pricked him with a thin needle and the air was slowly releasing from a puncture wound somewhere on his body. How much of a freakish coincidence could it be that Patrick had come to buy Henderson Manor? Surely, he had made some sort of mistake or jumped to conclusions. There had to be many women out there with the name, Zoe Henderson. Jenny didn't seem to think it was a coincidence, she was almost certain Patrick had gotten it right and that on some level, Sam was meant to meet Patrick because he would know what to do. Deborah, on the other hand, didn't believe a word that had come out of his mouth, even if she hadn't had the chance to meet him herself.

"There's no way he's telling the truth; he wants to suck money out of both of you," Deborah said as she handed Sam a hot coffee.

"But he said he wouldn't take any money from us," Jenny said as she sipped on a glass of wine.

"Of course he said that. He's not going to take anything off you straight away, is he? He'll *delve* a little deeper into it, and when his mind hits a *dead end*, so to speak, he'll then say he needs to charge you a fee."

Deborah was furious this had happened. How dare this Patrick person put Zoe into Sam's head? It had taken him long enough to forget her and what she had done to him.

"Deborah, I think this is all too close to be a coincidence," Jenny said. "I really think he's right and that he can help us."

"Are you seriously suggesting this flat is haunted?"

A wave of confusion crossed Jenny's face. How else would you explain it?

Deborah turned away from Jenny and looked into Sam's eyes. "Listen, baby, this is all nonsense, and the sooner you realise that, then the better off we'll all be."

Sam shook his head. He couldn't just leave things hanging like this. "No, something isn't right. And maybe this place isn't haunted or maybe Patrick has made a mistake. But until I know for sure, I can't let this lie." Sam stood up and went to his jacket hanging over the back of the single recliner across from the sofa.

"What are you doing?" Deborah asked.

"I'm phoning Patrick. I need to speak to him."

"But he's just left. See, look what he has done to you. You hear her name after all this time, and suddenly, you can't think of anything else."

Jenny nodded. "She's right, Sam. Leave it until tomorrow, when your head is a little clearer. You're a bit shaken because he told you it's Zoe."

"See, you said it yourself. *It's Zoe,* so you admit there is something going on in this flat, and there is a strong possibility it could have something to do with her."

Deborah tried to keep the venom from her voice as she spoke, but it was a hard task to carry out. "I'm sick of hearing *her* name. She's dead! How can she be doing any of this when all she is dust in the ground now?"

Sam ignored her and dialled. Deborah flapped her arms in the air in defeat and stormed into the kitchen.

"What's her problem?" Jenny asked quietly.

Jenny understood and agreed with Deborah's point, but at the same time, she wasn't the one to experience what had been happening in the flat, and she was also not around when Zoe was creating merry hell. Her thoughts were interrupted by Sam's voice.

"Patrick? It's Sam here. We need to talk. Can we meet?"

***

Patrick had sat Jodie down earlier that evening and explained everything. He was worried she would have gone crazy when she found out. What she had done was far worse.

"You seem really quiet. Are you okay?" Patrick asked her.

"I'm fine."

"Every man knows when his wife uses those words, it usually means the exact opposite."

Jodie didn't respond as she put Lewis's lunch for the next day into the fridge. Mashed up sweet potato with broccoli: he was a vegetable lover at a young age.

"Jodie, I can't ignore this. You do realise that?"

She didn't respond. Instead, she left the kitchen, went upstairs to their bedroom, and closed the door, leaving Patrick alone with his words.

Lying on the bed, she listened to Lewis's soft breathing and wondered what on earth Patrick had been thinking. How could he offer to bring his work home for a complete stranger and bring all this into Lewis's life?

He had explained to Jodie about Sam and how it had turned out they were living in the house of his ex, who was 'haunting' him and his flatmate. Jodie's response was flat and lifeless.

"You'll remember the night I was sleepwalking, when we first moved in? And I told you some spirit told me someone was missing, and they wanted my help to find them? Well, Zoe Henderson isn't in that plot. I think it's she who I've needed to find."

Jodie's response was relatively flat and lifeless. "Are you serious?"

"Jodie, I didn't ask for this; it's come around. You chose to leave this part of your life behind but I'm still very much a part of it."

"Did you not learn your lesson after what happened the last time?" Jodie had said as she stacked the dishwasher.

"That was different."

"Not so much. We lived in a different house then. It affected our personal life. I almost died at the hands of a lunatic. Why can't you see that you are tempting fate by getting involved in something like this again?"

Patrick had shaken his head at this point. "I'm not getting involved with a killer. I'm helping someone who is having trouble with something, and it turns out that it comes back to this house."

"Yes, this house!"

Jodie rarely lost her temper with Patrick, but when he was being stubborn to the point where it affected their son, then she wasn't going to stand back and be Little Miss Quiet.

"Jodie, it will be over before you know it."

"You know what, Patrick?" Jodie tried to calm herself. In anger, her emotions became jumbled and tears would flow, something she hated about herself. "I love you more than anything on this Earth, except for Lewis. And I'm *not* going to allow you to bring someone else's problems into this house and disrupt his little life just because their ex-lover used to live here. That's my final word on the matter."

They hadn't spoken much after the conversation, and Jodie had hoped her words had been strong enough for Patrick to understand she was dead against the idea.

As she lay on the bed, she propped herself up, resting the side of her face on her hand and watched Lewis as he slept in his cot. She knew he should be in his own room soon, but she couldn't bear the thought of him sleeping alone. The door opened slightly, and Patrick's head appeared in the gap.

"Can I come in?"

Without waiting for an answer, he entered the room. He caught a glimpse of his son asleep and knew what Jodie was asking was completely appropriate. However, something inside him didn't feel right when he considered ignoring it. Had his house not been at the centre of what was going on in Sam's flat, then it would be easy to pass it onto another medium. But it was, and so, he felt like he had to do something.

"We agreed after Ross we wouldn't let work life affect home life," Jodie said quietly.

"Yes, we did agree."

"So, what's changed?"

Patrick sat down on the bed, next to Jodie and without taking his eyes off his sleeping son. "This house and it's direct involvement with Sam. And it's for that reason I can't ignore it, Jodie."

Jodie sighed and fell back onto the pillow. "Patrick, if you bring this to our home, I will take Lewis, and I will not be back until you can prove to me we're your number one priority."

Patrick felt like he had been punched in the stomach. "Are you serious?"

Jodie could only nod.

Patrick stood up and slowly walked over to Lewis's cot. Watching his beautiful baby boy was the most tranquil feeling he had ever experienced, and his heart felt like it would burst with love and pride.

"Jodie, I think you and Lewis should leave, and when this is finished, you'll come back and things will be okay."

Jodie stood up and, feeling winded, couldn't think what to say.

"You're right. You and Lewis are my number one priority, and that's why you both shouldn't be in this house until I can sort things out. There are burial plots in our garden, for Christ's sake, and Sam is being harassed by his dead girlfriend who, funnily enough, used to live in this house. So, for both your safety and wellbeing, I think it's best you move out for a few days until I can get this sorted."

Jodie was still, with no words. "Are you serious?"

"I don't want you to go, Jodie. But you're right; you and Lewis can't be around this anymore. You have chosen to give up being a medium to be a mum to our beautiful boy, and I don't want to be the one who forces this on you."

Jodie opened the wardrobe next to Lewis's cot and pulled out two holdalls. She packed some items for herself but mostly Lewis's things.

"I'll help," Patrick said.

"No!"

Patrick stood back, feeling helpless. This house was supposed to be their new start, together as a family after what had happened with Ross.

Jodie must have been thinking the same thing.

"The only way we will ever work, Patrick, is if you give up the church too. We will only work if both our heads are at the centre of this family. It was okay before Lewis came along. But now that he's here, it's not okay for you to be working to help the dead and we're side-lined."

Patrick watched as Jodie packed the rest of the bags.

"I'll be at my parents until you've decided what you want more."

29

Sitting wallowing in his own pity was not something Patrick did often, however tonight, he felt, was an exception. He wondered what it was that he was doing. Jodie was gone from their home with their son, and all Patrick could think about was a stranger was being haunted by a spirit who had once lived in his house. He knew it was ridiculous, and that any other normal person would forget about it and get on with his own life, but Patrick felt a niggling in his stomach each time he tried to push it to the back of his mind. Would it have been better if they sold the house and moved somewhere else? A new build without any history, perhaps, or somewhere they could live in peace.

Patrick became distracted from his thoughts when he heard a sound from upstairs. He got up from the armchair in the sitting room and climbed the stairs. He was getting sick of this life, and not for the first time, he seriously considered giving up his place in the church. It wasn't worth all the hassle. He peered up to the landing and realised the loft hatch was open. Patrick knew he hadn't left it open. He jumped when the doorbell sounded and was opening the door before he knew it.

"Sam, come in."

Sam entered the house and stood still, memories flooding back to the last day he saw Zoe. "This place hasn't changed much."

"That's what having a baby does to your plans," Patrick replied.

"I don't really know what I'm doing here. But I had to come; gut instinct told me to."

Patrick nodded. "I know how that feels."

Patrick led Sam to the sitting room, having forgotten about the loft hatch. They sat down and were silent for a short time.

"It feels strange being back here." Sam broke the silence.

"I can imagine."

"The last time I saw her was in this room, you know."

Patrick eyed him as he spoke, wondering where this was leading. "That day didn't end well?"

Sam shook his head. His face was shadowed by a sadness that shouldn't have been there. He was with Deborah now, and he was happy. Things should have been getting better.

"You ever get that unsettling feeling that something's not right?"

"Yes," Patrick replied. "In fact, I have that feeling right now."

"You do?"

Patrick stood up and Sam followed.

"I know you probably don't understand what's going on in your flat right now, but I think I have a fair idea and considering your ex used to own this house and you've come here tonight, that tells me that you're willing to find out."

Sam nodded. "What are you thinking?"

Patrick walked towards the stairs. "If you want to find out for yourself and want my help, we have to do something you probably won't feel that comfortable with."

Sam felt sick, but he had to settle the feeling of uncertainty in his stomach. "I'll do anything to stop what's going on in my home."

***

As Patrick took his place across from Sam on the floor, Sam felt like his heart was trying to burst out from his chest. He could hear the blood in his ears rushing around as the adrenaline took over, and a feeling of fear and readiness flooded his veins.

"I can't believe I'm going to do this."

Patrick smiled, remembering his first experience of a séance. "Normally there are more people involved, but seeing as it's just the two of us, then we may as well get started."

"Will it work if it's just us?"

"So long as there is something that you need to know beyond what I can tell you, then, yes, it should work."

Sam took a deep breath and closed his eyes. Zoe Henderson's face flooded his mind. At first, she was smiling, the way she always used to before she changed.

I didn't change, Sam. Things changed.

Sam opened his eyes, expecting to see her standing right there in front of him. The only person who was in front of him was Patrick.

"I assume from your expression you heard that too?" Patrick asked him.

Sam didn't answer; instead, he thought it best to keep quiet and listen. He felt a change in the environment around him—it became colder, and his toes became icy.

You have to help her. She's lost!

A different voice this time that only Patrick could hear.

Sam continued to sit quietly and seemed to be in a trance, listening intently but he would only hear silence as the other voice filled Patrick's head.

Our girl needs your help. She has been accused of things which were not her fault.

Patrick opened his eyes to find Sam staring at him.

"I don't hear anything. Do you?"

Patrick closed his eyes, not willing to break the connection by speaking to him.

Zoe did not fall down those stairs. She was pushed!

Edith Henderson's voice was soft and clear, as if she were sitting right behind Patrick. She spoke with soft determination, and Patrick could feel her energy becoming stronger the longer he listened.

Our lovely granddaughter's life was taken needlessly. She was the only one left to carry on the family name. That chance was snatched away by someone who she loved and trusted.

Patrick did not reply as he listened to a voice to which the belonging corpse lay in his back garden in a family burial plot. No wonder Jodie had left.

You have to stop her before it's too late, and she hurts someone else.

Patrick wasn't sure where this was heading.

Zoe's time was forced upon her, and she's in limbo. She can't get to you to ask for help, since her energy is far too weak because she wasn't ready to go. That's why I'm here.

Patrick opened his eyes. Edith Henderson was in his line of sight. Her hair was white with very fine, auburn strands running through it. Her glasses were thick, big frames surrounding her eyes. Her voice certainly didn't match her appearance.

"Patrick?" Sam's voice snapped him back to reality.

"Sorry, I was miles away. What is it?"

"It's not Zoe who's been causing havoc in my flat, is it?"

Patrick frowned. "Why would you say that?"

Sam didn't know whether to smile or run. "Because I heard everything you did."

Patrick, Zoe was murdered. And by someone she knows.

Sam stood up and then climbed back down the loft hatch.

"Sam, wait!" Patrick called after him.

Patrick clambered down the loft hatch and was met by Sam's gaze. "You heard all of that?"

"Yes, I feel sick. How is it possible that, not only did I hear the voice of a dead old woman, but that Zoe was murdered?"

Patrick shook his head. "Maybe you're psychic?"

"Not funny."

Patrick closed the loft hatch and thought about the revelation they had both heard. "Who would want to murder Zoe?"

"Someone she knew, apparently. But I can't think of anyone. I never got to meet her friends and her family were all dead."

Back in the kitchen, Patrick opened two beers, and he and Sam sat at the table.

"I always found this house spooky," Sam said.

Patrick smiled, but it barely lifted the corners of his mouth. "Now you know why."

Sam looked around the kitchen and took in its vast size. The ceilings were so tall you would need a large ladder to reach them.

The place had such an old, vintage feel to it. With its size and lack of human occupancy, it should have felt empty. It didn't feel empty at all.

"Do you think a house like this can remember things?"

"Ha, you even sound like a psychic."

Sam stood up and walked to the door which led outside to the grounds of the house. As he looked out, he could see the headstones. He remembered Zoe showing him once, and it had scared him a little at first. But then, it made him think the house had a bit of character, something a lot of Glasgow's houses didn't have anymore. New builds were modern copycats of one another, with no feel to them. Sam had kind of grown to like the house before things had begun to go sour between him and Zoe.

"I mean, there is so much history inside this house. Do you think that because the Hendersons are the only family ever to have lived here, apart from you, they will always be here?"

Patrick considered this. "I think once Zoe has justice, the Henderson family will be just that: history. They will go off to wherever it is you go to when you die. They won't rest until Zoe's killer is behind bars."

30

Paul Preston had done nothing else but think about his retirement from the moment he had decided on a date. All he kept thinking of was himself and his wife Janet lying on the beach six weeks of the year while the sun would beat down, washing away any stresses they had. It was the only thing that would keep him going in the job. He only had six more months left as an officer, and he would be done. The only thing he would miss would be working with Jim. They had been partners for as long as he could remember, and Paul couldn't imagine he would have lasted as long as he had without Jim by his side. He savoured his annual leave, but he savoured his days on the job more—etching him closer to retirement.

Paul lay back on the reclining chair in his living room, relaxing after dinner. Janet had cleaned up the kitchen and gone out to the bingo with Barbara, who was Paul's new step mum. Janet teased him about it, but in all seriousness, Paul was glad his dad had found someone after his mum. Sadie had passed away from cancer five years previously.

Thomas Preston, also known to many as 'Auld Tam,' was in his seventies and full of life, more so than some people in their early twenties. He had been through a troublesome time since Sadie had died. At one point, Paul had worried his mum's death would kill his dad. He had sunken into himself and refused to go out or spend time with anyone, other than Paul. It was a wonder Tam had come to meet Barbara at all; they couldn't have been more opposite. Barbara was a full of life, easy going lady with a lot to give. When she had met Tam at a charity gig for cancer, she had seen something in him which was hiding and bursting to come out.

He had gone along to the gig only to support Paul, who had done a ten-kilometre run with other officers to raise money for Cancer Research. Paul and some of his colleagues were going to stand up and present the charity with a cheque for five thousand pounds. It had turned out Barbara was a volunteer fundraiser for the charity and got talking to Paul and Tam that evening. Tam would never have admitted to liking Barbara had it not been for Paul teasing him about it.

It was from then on Tam and Barbara had become companions. Paul and Janet had felt a wave of relief wash over them when they watched Tam return to his old self. He was socializing again, and before they knew it, he had moved in with Barbara at her house. She had even dragged him into the twenty-first century, and he was dressing with more style and using technology. He owned a smartphone, which Paul didn't even understand, and Tam was using social networking. He would keep in touch with old school friends through Facebook and seemed like the happy Tam everybody knew and loved.

Paul heard the front door open and a voice called through.

"Paul, are you in?" It was Tam, and he sounded jovial.

"In the living room, Dad."

Tam waltzed in and sat down on the couch, removing his hat and jacket.

"What you so cheery about?" Paul asked, failing to hide the smile from his face.

"Och, Barbara's only gone and won two grand at the bingo!" He slapped his thigh as he chuckled away.

Paul's eyes widened. "Are you kidding?"

"I widnae joke aboot something like that, son. It's nae good tae dae that tae the heart."

Paul stood up and walked over to his dad. He held out his hand and helped Tam up from the couch. "This deserves a wee dram, don't you think?"

Tam rubbed his hands together. "Aye, noo yer talking, son, noo yer talking."

They walked into the kitchen, and Paul pulled out a chair from the dining table, where Tam took his place. Paul opened the drinks cupboard and pulled out a bottle of whisky and two glasses. As he approached the table, Tam was tapping away on his phone.

"Who are you texting now?" Paul asked.

"Barbara. I'm suggesting a night away at that fancy hotel doon next to the bridge. What dae ye call it again?"

Paul shook his head as he laughed. "Too expensive, that's what I call it. Why do you want to go there anyway?"

"My beautiful lady has just won two grand. What else would we be spending it on?"

Paul poured the whisky into the glasses and passed one across the table to his dad. It was great to see him so happy.

"Other than winning at the bingo, what else have you and Barbara been doing?"

Tam sipped at the whisky and savoured the flavour. The warmth of the liquid trickled down his throat, and he let out a gasp of pleasure as it did so. "Uck, no much son. Ye know, at oor age we're glad we're still breathin', eh."

"Nice and morbid, Dad. Thanks for that."

Tam chuckled away to himself as Paul poured more whisky into their glasses. "Aye, well ye never know. I mean, look at wee Rab—he died just the other day there. Dropped doon deed while he wiz eating a fish supper. Poor auld bugger."

Paul almost spat his whisky back into the glass. "Wee Rab died?"

"Aye son, did a no tell ye? Uck sorry aboot that, time gets away fae ye at this age. I must've forgot."

Paul was in disbelief. Wee Rab had been his dad's neighbour since Paul had been a little boy, and he was one of the nicest men you could ever meet. "I can't believe it. How did you find out?"

"Norma phoned to tell me. She's cut up, the poor soul. She went tae get him a napkin fae the kitchen, and when she got back, he'd collapsed on the floor. Died fae a heart attack."

Paul practically threw the whisky down his throat and poured another one. "When's the funeral?"

"Monday, ye going?"

Paul nodded. "Should pay my respects. I've known the man since I was a wee boy. Poor Rab, poor Norma."

Tam nodded and finished his whisky. They heard a key in the door.

"Dad?" a voice called.

"Uck, wee Janey's here."

"Grampa?" Jane replied.

Jane Preston appeared in the kitchen doorway with a big grin. "Hi, Grampa, nice to see you. How are you?"

"Barbara won at bingo."

Jane hugged her dad as she spoke to Tam. "Oh really? That's great. How much?"

"Two grand, apparently," Paul answered.

Jane whistled. "Nice one."

Tam got up from his seat. "Excuse me, nature calls."

As Tam left the room, Paul put the whisky back in the cupboard. It was too early in the day to drink the rest.

Jane sensed the tension. "Dad, what's wrong?"

"Your Grampa just told me that Wee Rab died."

Jane frowned. "Who's that?"

Paul shook his head and led them into the living room. "Never mind, I'll tell you about it later."

***

Tam switched the bathroom light off and as he walked passed the room to his left, he saw the computer sitting on the desk, which Jane often used for her university course work. He walked into the room and switched it on. Tam had been terrified of technology before meeting Barbara and had no idea how anyone could work anything remotely more challenging than a typewriter. As he waited for the computer to load up, he looked around the room and saw pictures of his family dotted on the walls.

There were photos of his wedding day to his late wife Liz, photos of his granddaughters, Jane and Lisa, and various holiday snaps. They made him smile. It was good to see Liz in a photo smiling; it helped him to forget the pain he had seen her in when she had been suffering from cancer.

The screen lighting up distracted him from the photos, and he clicked on the internet icon. Google Chrome filled the screen and Tam typed into the search bar to find Facebook. As he clicked on it, he searched his mind for his log in details. However, he found that Facebook was already logged into someone else's page.

"Jane, ye forgot tae log oot ya silly girl. Fraudsters are all over the internet, don't ye know," Tam said under his breath as he looked at Jane's profile picture.

As he moved the mouse up to the log out icon, he noticed something that wasn't right. His eyes scanned the screen further, and he found the name didn't match his granddaughter's photo.

He clicked on the photo album and found photos of Jane with a man around the same age as her. He didn't recognise the male in the picture and the 'about' section was nothing to do with Jane.

"Grampa, what are you doing in here?" Jane asked.

"Oh, jeezo, Jane. You scared me half tae death there!"

Jane walked over to the computer screen, peering over Tam's shoulder.

"Jane, I think there's something wrong with Facebook. It's your picture, but the name isn't yours."

Jane nodded. "It's for university, I've created a character page for one of my projects. Don't worry, Grampa. I haven't been hacked or anything."

Tam stood up from the computer chair and smiled. "Awe, that's a'right, then. For a minute there, I was thinking, who the hell is Deborah Bell?" Tam laughed as he walked out the room. "Just a'ways mind an' log oot. Ye never know who's trawlin' the internet, hen."

Jane returned his smile. "Will do, Grampa."

"Shit!"

31

*I*t's only a matter of time now. I mean, what am I going to do when it all comes out? Maybe I can take off somewhere and not come back. But how can I leave him? How can I leave them? This is all one big mess.

"You fancy a cup of tea, Jane?" my mum asked as I stared at the television.

"No, thanks. I'm going to head out now."

My mum just smiled. She was the loveliest mum on the planet. This was going to kill her when she found out. It would be a lot easier if I wasn't in love with him, or if I was one of those people who was devoid of emotion. To be perfectly honest, I don't even know how I got to this place. It was meant to be a one-night thing, where I could fulfil my lust for someone and move on. But from the minute he kissed me, I was hooked on him: his scent, his touch, his voice, everything that he stood for.

"That's me away, Dad."

"Okay, love, you be safe. There are a lot of bad people out there."

I smirked inside.

There it goes again, that part of me that I hate. It can hide from me for months at a time, then it rears its ugly head when I least expect it. I hate that part of me. And if I hate it, others certainly will when it presents itself, which it will, eventually.

"I know how to protect myself, Dad. It pays to have a high-up-in-the-force officer as a dad."

He kissed me on the forehead, and I heard Lisa call down from the bedroom.

"See you soon, Jane."

"Bye!"

My Grampa Tam tried to stand up, but I stopped him.

"Don't get up."

I bent down and hugged him tight. It killed me he had found that Facebook profile. It killed me he thinks of me as someone kind, loving and upstanding. If only he knew, if only all of them knew.

"Have a good night, hen. Look after yersel."

I put my coat on and pulled my phone out of my bag. I had three missed calls from Sam. I wondered what was wrong. It had to be something; last time I saw him he said, he was going to see that bloody psychic, Patrick something.

"Bye!" I called before I closed the front door.

I was out in the night, on my own, and to be honest, to have so many good people in my life, I had never felt so alone. I was scared of the person I had become. I mean, what happened to Zoe was… crazy. I hadn't planned it, and I had never wanted to physically hurt her, or anyone else for that matter.

But when it came to Sam, no one could understand how much it hurt. To watch him, hear him with someone else. I know it started off as a silly crush, after watching him as an actor in small time telly shows and stage shows. I was on placement in the theatre, and I couldn't take my eyes off him. He never noticed me, not once. Then, all of a sudden, mine and my sister's best friend drops the bombshell that she's going out with him. I mean, how the hell did that happen?

I was distraught; my heart wasn't only broken, but shattered. It was one thing to know he might have a girlfriend, but to know it was my best friend and hear all the sordid details of their sex life and how much he treated her like a princess, that was something else entirely. It was then that something inside me snapped. All I wanted was Sam, and at that precise moment, I didn't care who got hurt in the process; so long as it wasn't me. I began doing things that would put a strain on their relationship. I listened intently to how Zoe had been a little jealous of Jenny, and how she found it strange Sam could be so close to another female and not have feelings or find her attractive. I listened as she explained to Lisa and how she had briefly spoken to Sam about her feelings, and he had assured her it was nothing to worry about.

Then, I had an idea. What if I implemented something that would split them up, something that would keep them apart forever? So, I started to do things that would make Zoe look like a crazy jealous girlfriend. I took photographs of Sam with Jenny, looking happy and 'couple' like. I also took photos of Sam and Zoe together, Sam on his own, doing his own thing. I sent letters, messages, and all sorts of stuff that made it look like Zoe had been stalking her own boyfriend. It drove them both crazy. So much so that he ended it with her.

I had been in her house when it happened. I heard the whole thing. I got excited when I heard him tell her it was over, and she screamed and cried like a stupid, needy little bitch. Not only did I get excited, but I was also scared to death at the person I had become. But I couldn't stop myself. It was like an obsession. It was then the whole situation got out of control, and my plan strayed from a breakup mission to something far worse.

***

My hands stayed in the position they had taken to push Zoe down the stairs. I say push…she sort of fell. When she asked me to leave, all I wanted to do was shut her up, tell her she would never have Sam the way she wanted, and that he didn't want her anymore. But I didn't say it. I just looked her in the eye, and she could tell I was smug about something.

She had come into the bedroom once Sam had left and saw me standing at the window, watching him walk away; she looked confused to see me there.

"What are you doing here?" she asked.

"I've come to see if you're okay?" I replied. "You've not been around much."

Zoe looked at me with sadness in her eyes, "I suppose you heard all of that."

I smiled gently. "Yes, are you okay?"

"No, I'm not. He won't listen. He thinks I've been stalking him and his friend Jenny," she said.

I frowned. "How can you stalk your own boyfriend?"

Zoe was pacing the floor. Her eyes were a picture of crazed devastation. "You tell me how I can stalk my own boyfriend. Jesus, I wouldn't know where to bloody start."

I watched her as she paced back and forth, her brow glistened with sweat, and I swear I could hear her heart banging around inside her chest. She stopped suddenly and looked in my direction. "How did you get in here?"

I hadn't thought of this one. *Shit!*

"I asked you a question."

I remained calm, "The door was open. I did knock, but there was no answer, so I tried the door and it opened. I assumed you were in. I didn't think you'd leave a house this size open for all and sundry to waltz in."

"Like you did, you mean?"

I couldn't risk her finding out what I had been doing so I had to try to sway the subject back to Sam being unreasonable in thinking Zoe had been stalking him. "You think that it was Jenny? Maybe she was jealous of you and Sam?"

She didn't reply to my suggestion. She was quiet. Too quiet; she was thinking.

"What is it, Zoe?" I asked, but still, she remained silent.

I watched her as she sat on the edge of her bed, and I could see that her brain was working overtime. I was frozen. It was like time had been paused, and the only people exempt from it were her and I.

After what felt like a lifetime, she looked at me with caution. She rose from the foot of her bed; I was still standing at the window. Her voice was almost a whisper.

"Oh my god, I can't believe I haven't worked it out before now."

"What are you talking about?" I asked curiously.

"It's you. You're the one who's been stalking him."

"Don't be so bloody ridiculous!" I spat.

She walked towards me slowly, eyeing me from head to toe. "It's not ridiculous. It makes perfect sense."

I laughed. "And how the hell do you work that one out?"

"When I told you who I was going out with, you couldn't have been more critical. You said things like, 'He's only after one thing.' 'He'll drop you for some theatre star.' 'He's not that perfect, and he'll break your heart.' And when I told you I thought I had fallen for him, you couldn't even look at me."

My heart pounded, and my head throbbed. My palms had become clammy, and all I wanted was to slap her in the face and get out of there, but my instinct told me to remain cool and deal with what was coming.

Zoe smiled, and her eyes sparkled with the tears that were filling them yet again. "You're the one who has been sending the notes and photographs. You're clever, I'll give you that. I don't know how you've done it, but you have."

She clapped sarcastically. I was angry, and I couldn't tell if it was with her or that she had rumbled me. She had figured out what I had been doing, and in all honesty, I hated that she was being so smug and proud about it. I felt a burning desire in my stomach; it rose to my chest and then to my throat, like I would explode. But I pushed it deep down, back to its pit. I wanted to launch myself at her, kill her right there and then. But I couldn't bring myself to move. So all I said was, "So what if it was me?"

She shook her head. She couldn't take her eyes off mine, as if she was searching for answers, for the friend she once knew. Then, she asked, "Why didn't you tell me how you felt?"

I was stunned. Zoe sounded sad, not at all smug as I had initially thought. What could I say? Why *had* I done this? Even I wasn't sure how to explain it.

"Because I could." The words were out of my mouth before I had even thought of them.

Zoe walked to the door. My emotions were all over the place—I couldn't decide if I felt guilty, sad or pissed off.

"I still don't get why you're here?"

"I wanted to hear him tell you to get out of his life!" I snarled. I was surprising myself at how nasty I had become.

Zoe suddenly lost it; she screamed through gritted teeth. She ran at me quickly as I stood at the window and grabbed me by the arm. "Get the fuck out my house before I phone the police and have you done for harassment!"

I pulled my arm from her grip and slapped her across the face. The stupid bitch had no idea what was about to happen, and neither did I.

"Listen, Zoe, you do anything of the sort, and I *will* kill you, understood?" I hissed.

Zoe took no notice and grabbed my arm again, this time with more force and dragged me out to the top landing of the hallway, all the while laying blows down on my head and shoulders. "I said out!" she screamed again. "You were supposed to be my friend, and this is how you treat me. You're a psycho!"

I managed to shake her off and pushed her away. I hadn't meant to push her down the stairs; I couldn't see where we were positioned on the landing, because I was trying to protect myself from the raining blows to my head. I hadn't even seen her fall; I only heard it. She thumped down, gravity pulling at her all the way to the bottom. No sounds or pleas came from her throat. I only looked up when my conscience told me something was wrong. When I did, I was horrified at what I saw. A twisted neck, a badly broken leg (I only knew it was broken from the angle in which it positioned itself once the body was still) and open eyes.

For a few moments, I was thinking, *Shit! I've killed her.*

And then, as I looked on at the badly positioned corpse, I thought, *Hang on, this is what I wanted; her out of the way.*

My advantage was that nobody had seen me enter the house, so straight away, I won't be able to be placed here visually. Second advantage was that I had stashed everything in a box under her bed.

The hate mail, the notes, photographs of Jenny and of Sam. A list of dates, times and places where Jenny had been with Sam, all of which were beautifully crafted by me, someone who had never met these people in person, and the mobile phone used to send the messages. I had taken their numbers from Zoe's phone one evening when she had first started seeing Sam. I knew they would suspect her and Zoe would suspect Jenny. I was careful of my ways. I obviously couldn't have handwritten the notes, as that may have caused me problems. I made sure all of those were typed on a computer that couldn't be traced back to me. Third advantage; I had made damn sure I would not leave any prints behind, so I wore the black leather gloves Sam had given Zoe as a gift, which she had raved about. Looks like they came in use for something other than winter. I'd stolen them from her on the night that I had taken Sam and Jenny's numbers from Zoe's phone. I needed something he had touched, something that would smell of him and would allow me to feel a little closer to him.

I decided this was a blessing in disguise and what had been done couldn't be changed. So, I slowly made my way down the stairway. I stepped over her body and took a last look before I made my way to the back door. She looked uncomfortable once she was dead. Her frame all twisted and out of shape; she must've bounced off every stair and piece of banister on her descent to have been looking like she was once she reached the bottom.

I knew it was not possible, but she looked through me with those dead eyes. I hadn't thought about it before, what it would feel like to be stood over the body of the person I had killed. I didn't *mean* to push her down the stairs, I meant to push her away from me, and then, she accidentally fell down the stairs. Either way, I had to leave. I couldn't risk being here a minute longer.

I bent down to have a closer look at her face, I guess you could say curiosity got the better of me. I had never been that close to a corpse before. Her eyes were glazed over, however there was a look of terror on her face. She must have known she was going to die as she tumbled down.

I thought I would do the decent thing and provide Zoe with the smallest amount of dignity and close her eyes, of course ensuring I kept the gloves on.

I had the most horrid thought she would jump up and finish me off, and it almost stopped me from doing it. Of course, she didn't, although I did have an unnerving feeling. Yes, I knew I had just killed someone, but I couldn't help feeling the hairs on my neck prick up when I touched her face. It was almost as if she was telling me she was still there. My irrational thoughts quickly dispersed as I realised I would never have to deal with that woman again as long as I lived. And neither would Sam.

As I stood up, I looked around for any evidence that would have indicated my presence but couldn't point anything out, so I took a deep breath and made my way to the back door.

I slipped out unseen and made my way home. Sam's nightmare, as far as he was concerned, was over. He had ended things with Zoe, and then, I killed her. But no one would know about that; no one could ever know.

My brain was in overdrive as I walked home. Everything I had done in the last few months was because of my desire to split up Sam and Zoe. She asked me why I didn't tell her how I felt. I had to be honest with myself and admit I couldn't answer that question. I really didn't know why I hadn't told her. It could've been the fear of rejection on her part or the fear of embarrassment. Whatever the hidden reason, it didn't matter, because Zoe was lying at the bottom of the stairs in that huge house, as dead as I was alive, and for some strange reason, I felt nothing. Nothing for Zoe but absolutely every feeling that's possible for a human to feel, towards Sam.

It was true, I was in love with Sam and I always had been, ever since Zoe met him. It was a crush at first from all of his TV and theatre work. I could always handle my feelings when it was just a crush, when he was some actor on the stage. But when I found out he was going out with my lovely friend Zoe, something inside me changed. I instantly changed the way I felt about my friendship with Zoe, and I couldn't stop the overwhelming feeling of wanting to see her suffer.

I knew my love was stronger than any other kind out there, as I'd never heard anyone talk about their feelings the way I knew my own. At first, I tried to suppress these feelings, because I knew in my heart and in my head they were not healthy. But as time went on and my feelings for Sam grew, they began to burst out of me. I couldn't tell anyone; I didn't think that anyone would understand it.

If my feelings had been visible to the human eye, I'd imagined they would look like a huge rainbow rising from my chest. As time went on, some of those beautiful rainbow colours which I imagined pouring out of me turned to a dark, not so pleasant shade. A shade which made me understand my feelings were beyond love. I had become unhealthy in my feelings for Sam. You might go as far as to say I had become obsessed.

I was not proud of what I did to Zoe, but I was certainly not ashamed either. I was only doing what was best for the good of my heart. It was aching to see him with a potential future partner that wasn't me, even if it was my best friend. And she was my best friend for a while, but I had to do something to scare her away.

You see, I hadn't ever *planned* to kill anyone. All I wanted was for Sam to notice me and perhaps fall for me the way I had fallen for him. I wanted him to be happy, but I couldn't bear the thought of him being with anyone else.

I could never let that happen.

So now you'll understand what happened to Claire Prowse.

32

I put the key in the door of Sam and Jenny's flat and paused before I turned it. What if that stupid psychic had put ideas in Sam's head? What if he had begun to suspect me?

"Don't be so ridiculous," I whispered to myself as I turned the key and opened the door.

I entered an empty flat; how comforting it was to know he was still with the psychic. I switched on the light and almost jumped out of my skin when I saw my own reflection in the mirror on the bottom wall facing the door. All this psychic talk was freaking me out. I dumped my handbag in Sam's room and went into the kitchen to switch the kettle on. I saw a bottle of wine sitting in the wine rack and decided it looked more appealing than a mug of hot water with a tea bag floating around inside it. I reached up to retrieve a glass when I heard the front door open.

"Hello?" Sam's voice was smooth as silk as it floated through to the kitchen.

"Hi, do you fancy a glass of wine?" I called back.

I looked up to see his anguished face in the doorway. He nodded in reply.

"What's wrong?" I asked.

Sam pulled me into his arms and held me close, so close in fact I felt like I was going to pop. "I went to Patrick's house."

I pulled away and looked up at the beautiful face which was tormented by his dead ex-girlfriend. How could she still be in my way when she was dead? "And?" was all I could manage, but with a positive tone behind it.

"Did I mention he has bought Zoe's old house?" Sam's eyes searched mine, though I was not so sure what for.

"Small world, eh?" Shit! Of all the houses in Glasgow, the psychic had to buy fucking Henderson Manor.

"He's pretty sure he can figure out what's going on in this flat, and he's certain it's something to do with Zoe." He released me from his embrace and opened the bottle of wine. "You having one?"

I nodded. I listened to the glugging sound from the bottle, and when he finished pouring mine, I gulped a large mouthful down.

"Deborah, it's not going out of fashion." He laughed as he watched me.

I smiled. Why couldn't I speak? He was going to get suspicious. I had to change the subject. "Let's put the telly on and get more comfortable with that wine."

He smiled and followed me into the lounge. I felt his strong presence behind me and wished everything and everyone could just disappear. I switched on the television, and the news was starting. We settled down on the couch, and Sam draped his arm over me. I settled a little more now.

A recap of the recent headlines: it is thought that the woman's body recently discovered in the West End is the product of murder. She was found to have one knife wound to the neck and was discovered by a young teenage dog walker at around six o'clock yesterday morning. She has now been named as twenty-five-year-old Claire Prowse. Police are appealing for witnesses.

"Isn't that the girl who works in that café around the corner?" I heard Sam's voice distantly.

"I don't know," I said, trying to hide the dryness in my voice.

Just as the words were out of my mouth, there it was filling the screen: Claire Prowse's face.

"I thought it was her. Jesus Christ, that's a shocker."

I watched as the reporter went on to give more detail about the circumstances surrounding her death, but I didn't hear anything. It was as if I had suddenly gone deaf.

"How could someone do something so callous?" I said, with as much emotion as I could push into the words.

"I know, it's awful; to think that she served us food not so long ago. She was really friendly," Sam said.

I know, I thought. *I remember how friendly she was, and how cocky she had been when we were in the bathroom of that restaurant; hence the reason she's bloody dead.*

We heard the front door open, and the sound of Jenny's high heels tottering down the hall.

"Hey! Ooh, wine." Her eyes widened and so did her smile as soon as she saw our glasses.

"The bottle's in the kitchen," I said, welcoming the distraction.

"Hey, Jenny; you remember that Claire girl from the café around the corner?" Sam called after her.

My stomach was lurching, and I felt my head throb. This wasn't happening. I couldn't keep up the pretence much longer. I was pretending to be someone else to keep hold of my man. What the hell was I doing?

"Yeah, why?" Jenny was suddenly in the lounge clutching at a large glass of wine.

"She was murdered yesterday."

Jenny looked at the television and then back to Sam. "What the hell happened?"

"A knife wound to the neck, apparently," I added. I didn't want to seem too quiet, or they would get suspicious. *I* would be suspicious of me. What was I thinking about? Of course this would be on the news. But it's okay, because I wore protection. I wore the same gloves I was wearing when I killed Zoe. So, my prints wouldn't be accounted for. It was strange for me to think about how I had killed Zoe, and I had been wearing a pair of gloves which Sam had given to her as a gift.

"What the hell is the world coming to, when a girl can't walk down the street for fear of being stabbed in the neck? I know I wasn't the nicest person in the world to her, but no one deserves that," Jenny said, shaking her head in disgust before sipping at her wine.

We watched the rest of the news in silence, and I tried to stop my shoulders from tensing. I couldn't believe we were sitting together, watching the news of a girl who had been murdered by *me*, and my boyfriend and my friend were none the wiser.

Yes, Jenny and I *had* become friends as I had spent so much of my time at their flat. The more time I'd spent there, the more I had come to realise Jenny was no threat. Of course, I knew she wasn't a threat; I was the one who had created that illusion, but with Sam having become so precious to me, I couldn't help but worry that someone, anyone, could have snatched him away at any point. I would go as far as to say she was one of my closest friends. But I knew all of this was a lie, all of it. The only truth was my unconditional love for Sam. I didn't think there was anything on this earth he could do that would make me second guess my love for him. If he told me he had murdered someone in cold blood, I genuinely think I would be okay to move past it. But I knew there was no way he would feel the same. If he knew what I had done, what I'd done to be with him, then he would cut all ties with me.

I had to remind myself this little fantasy story I was living would be coming to an end relatively soon. Sam knew me as Deborah Bell, mysterious and fun. I hadn't ever given him the opportunity to meet my family because there was absolutely no way around it. I mean, how the hell would I explain firstly that my name was not my name? And secondly, Lisa would instantly figure everything out. My sister was like my dad in that sense — she had traits of being a good detective and not a lot of things got past her. That's why I had kept all of this a secret. I didn't mention anything about a relationship with anyone. The only thing I ever mentioned was my friend from university. I didn't divulge any information about how I met her, who she was, or where she was from. That would have been too dangerous. She would have worked it out in a second, even though she had never met Sam when he was with Zoe.

Zoe had told her so much she would have put two and two together.

My head was spinning from it all, and even though I watched the screen, I was not listening to the words spoken by the reporter.

"I think I'm going to head to bed. The wine has muddled with me," I said, smiling.

"Okay, I'll be in soon. I want to watch the rest of this and see if there is anything else on Claire," Sam said.

I felt sick.

"Okay, goodnight." I bent down to kiss him and then went to Sam's bedroom.

I undressed as I sat on my side of his bed and looked at the little photo in the frame of us together. Jenny had taken it; we had been sitting in the kitchen having dinner when she took it. It was my favourite thing to look at if I was feeling sad or scared, except for the real thing, of course.

I crawled under the quilt and lay my head on the pillow. Memories of the night I killed Claire swirled around in my mind. She hadn't even seen me coming; she was walking along the car park on her way home from work. It had all happened so quickly. I had taken a knife from Sam's kitchen and gone to the café to wait for her in the shadows. Sounded sinister I knew, but I had to do something. She was too friendly, and I knew that guys like Sam might read the signs wrong — especially Sam. He was so lovely, and he would read her signs of lust and passion as signs of friendship and end up in a compromising situation. What had really done it was the conversation in the bathroom in that café. The stupid bitch hadn't realised what I was capable of.

Claire didn't protest. She didn't shout out or plead. It was quick and easy, which scared me. It scared me how easy it was and how much of a thrill it gave me. Her life was in my hands, and it was up to me whether she lived or died. I chose the latter. There was no choice really; I had to do it for the good of my heart. I knew what I was doing was wrong, and I would be caught eventually, but until that day was upon me, I would do anything to keep Sam in my life. I knew it would hurt him when he found out what I was, who I really was.

As I drifted off, I felt the bed dip on Sam's side. I smiled gently at the thought of him cuddling in to me and falling asleep.

"Night baby," I said sleepily.

I felt his arm slide around me over the top of the quilt, and I felt his breath on my ear.

Not long now, Jane.

The words that were whispered harshly into my ear made me jump out of the bed. When I turned to face the bed, Sam's side was empty. It was then I realised the voice was female.

Zoe Henderson wasn't going to let me forget what I had done to her. And I was sure she wasn't going to let me forget about Claire either.

33

S am woke up to find he was no longer sharing his bed with Deborah, and she had left a note on his bedside table. It read; *Gone shopping, will be back soon. Love you. D x*

Sam stretched out and got out of bed. The room was cold, and so he put on a pair of tracksuit bottoms and a T-shirt. He yawned and on exhaling, he saw a white mist appear in front of his face. Was it *so* cold he could see his breath? He was startled by the crash behind him, and when he turned back to face the bed, he saw a photo frame on the floor, face down with broken glass surrounding it.

"What the hell was that?" he found himself asking.

He picked up the frame and inspected the area around it. There was nothing that could have knocked it over. There was no breeze, and he was nowhere near it.

Something made him look up at the mirror on his dresser, and he drew back in fear of the face staring back at him. Zoe Henderson.

You're one big fool, Sam.

Sam watched as the eyes became narrow on Zoe's face as she looked out at him. Her mouth did not move, but he heard the words. What did she mean?

Sam closed his eyes and hoped when he opened them, she would be gone. He felt himself shiver, and as he opened his eyes, he was relieved to see she was gone. Sam got dressed quickly and grabbed his phone and the photo frame. He searched for the name in the phone's address book and pressed the call button.

"Patrick, it's Sam. I'm coming over. I have something to show you."

"You sound shaken up. Are you okay?"

Sam exited his building and was halfway down his street already. He didn't want to be in his flat any longer than he had to.

"Not really. I'll be with you in about fifteen minutes. I'm getting in a taxi now."

Sam ended the call and told the driver where to go. All the while, he clutched at the photo frame and replayed Zoe's words over and over in his head.

***

Sam walked up the gravel driveway towards the main entrance to Henderson Manor. His eyes scanned the entire building and thought about Zoe's death. What a lonely way to die. He found himself outside the door, and before he could ring the bell, Patrick opened the door wide and invited him inside. Without saying a word, Sam handed the photo frame to Patrick.

"What's this?"

"It's a picture of me and my girlfriend, Deborah."

Patrick frowned. "Why would I want to see this in such a hurry? No offence."

Sam turned away from the stairs to face Patrick. "Because when I woke up this morning, alone, it was knocked off my bedside table with such force it smashed."

Sam searched Patrick's face for answers.

"There's no way you could've knocked it over by yourself?"

Sam laughed loudly. "So, *you're* a sceptic as well as a psychic?"

Patrick shook his head and looked down at the photo. "Who did you say the girl in the picture is?"

"Deborah. My girlfriend."

Patrick walked to the kitchen, and Sam followed him, not daring to look at the bottom of the stairs. He had a horrible feeling he would see Zoe lying there, and he was already feeling guilty about her death.

"Zoe's death wasn't your fault, Sam. You didn't kill her."

"Someone else did, though. I think she's trying to tell me something about it. Why else would my flat have all these weird things happening in it?"

Sam looked up from the floor as Patrick sat down at the kitchen table. Patrick wasn't looking at Sam; he was studying the photo.

"This must have come down with some force for it to have broken into shards like it has."

Sam was quiet for a moment. He tried to put into order the words he wanted to say. "Zoe was in my bedroom this morning, straight after that frame was knocked down. She spoke to me, but her lips didn't move. It was like I heard her voice in my head."

Patrick nodded. "That's the way it normally goes. What did you hear?"

"She said I was a fool."

Patrick was quiet.

"What's wrong?"

"I think you're right. I think Zoe is trying to tell you something about her death."

Sam sat across from Patrick. He feared the outcome of the events leading him to Patrick. "So, what do we do about it? I mean, this concerns both of us. After all, this used to be her house."

Patrick put the photo frame to one side and thought for a moment. He couldn't sort this alone. If Zoe was murdered, he had to involve the police. He knew the outcome of her death was concluded as accidental because Sam had explained it all to him. Patrick knew it wasn't accidental, but he had to find a way of proving it to his sources.

"I have connections in the police. I'll contact them today and see if they'll entertain me."

Sam sat back and seemed to relax at Patrick's words. "You think they'll listen?"

"They have in the past. I can't say for sure that they will again. You don't ask; you don't get."

34

DS Paul Preston and DC Jim Lang were sat in the office, doing the least enjoyable part of the job: paperwork. If they had picked a job that was purely office based, they would have died of boredom long ago.

"My dad came over last night after dinner," Preston attempted to fill the silence.

"Oh, aye?"

"Seems Barbara won big at the bingo."

Jim Lang laughed. Knowing Tam well enough, he could tell what was coming next. "I assume he wanted her to spend big on him?"

The shrill ringing of the phone pierced their ears, and as Preston reached for the receiver, he said, "Aye, he wanted to book them into some posh hotel down next to the Erskine Bridge."

Lang smiled and shook his head as Preston turned his voice to that of a professional.

"DS Preston speaking."

Lang continued shuffling papers and busying himself when one word made him look up.

"Patrick."

Lang narrowed his eyes and mouthed, "What does he want?"

"The Zoe Henderson case was closed last year, Patrick."

Lang frowned.

"By all means, although I'm not sure how I can…" Preston pulled the receiver away from his face and stared at it.

"That was weird."

"What did he want?" Lang asked.

"He wants to talk to us about Zoe Henderson."

"Why?

Preston shook his head. "He said he has some information that may contribute to her case."

Lang stood up and walked over to the whiteboard in the office. They didn't have time to be mucking around with this ghostly nonsense again. There had been a brutal and callous murder, and the last thing Lang wanted was Patrick hanging around saying the poor girl had come to him in his sleep or some other crap like that.

"Unless he's brought her back to life, I doubt there is anything we can do for him. What's he got to do with her anyway?"

"God knows, but he sounded pretty certain on the phone."

Preston and Lang had been working on the Claire Prowse case over the last few days and had hit a brick wall with the lack of evidence. There had been no murder weapon, no prints at the scene; nothing. Her face stared out at them from the whiteboard in the office, and Lang wondered, like he always did, how people could be so cruel, for such a young girl to die in such a brutal way baffled him.

"It would be more helpful if he had a lead on the bloody Prowse case. That's what we need right now." Lang said through gritted teeth.

"Her phone records should be back by the end of the day, and the CCTV from the café where she worked should provide us with information on the people she had come into contact with over the last few weeks. If we spot the same person more than once, we need to speak to them."

"And the CCTV from the street cameras?" Lang asked.

"That should be back at the same time as the footage from the café."

Lang turned his back on the whiteboard and exhaled loudly, demonstrating his frustration. "I'll grab us some coffee; we're going to need it if Mr McLaughlin will be joining us."

Some things never change, Preston thought.

***

Patrick walked into the station and felt a wave of déjà vu wash over him. He was transported back to the first time he walked through the doors of Pitt Street Police Station and remembered feeling scrutinized by Lang and not quietly by any means. He remembered the worrying look on Jodie's face when he had told her he was going to the station to tell the police about his knowledge of the murders of the girls in the city centre. He still thought about them from time to time. Patrick remembered how he felt when he imagined what it would have been like not to help them but to ignore them. It would have niggled away at him, and their families would never have found justice.

That was how he felt walking into the station now, that niggling feeling in the back of his mind. Jodie had been so supportive the last time that it had almost killed her. Ross had almost killed her. Patrick tried not to think about that part of his life and what it may have been like had he not been adopted. It made him sick to his stomach. His mind was asking him if what he was doing was the right thing for him, for his family. Jodie had walked away with Lewis, the two people in his life who he would take a bullet for, yet they were gone, and here he found himself standing in a police station, once again fighting for the dead instead of the living. He could not stop himself. Patrick could feel it in his gut what he was doing was the right thing for the long term, although he could not explain how. He knew Jodie and Lewis would be waiting for him when all this was over with. He just didn't know how long it would take.

"I'm here to see DS Preston and DC Lang," he said to the officer behind the desk.

Patrick waited for a few moments before he was greeted by Lang.

"Patrick, long time no see." Lang offered his hand.

Patrick shook his hand and then followed Lang back to his and Preston's office. Walking down the corridor took him back to that day again; where he bared his soul to the two officers for the first time and remembered how Lang was having none of it. Preston had been kinder to Patrick and was willing to listen. He had the sneaking suspicion that history would repeat itself.

Lang opened the office door and allowed Patrick to go inside first.

"Patrick, nice to see you. To what do we owe this pleasure?" Preston stood up from his seat.

He heard the door close behind him, sure he felt Lang's eyes burn into the back of his head. They all sat down, and Patrick tried to figure out how to place his words.

Lang eyed Patrick with scrutiny, like he had the first time they had met.

"You investigated the murder of Zoe Henderson last year."

Preston nodded.

"And her death was concluded as accidental," Lang added, with certainty.

"I bought her house earlier this year."

Again, Preston was silent. However, he heard a loud sigh come from Lang. "Oh course you did."

"And what do you mean by that?" Patrick replied, failing to hide his annoyance towards Lang's ever so sceptic attitude.

"Gentlemen, it's like old times," Preston shook his head. "Patrick, unless you have something concrete that would make us consider looking into the death of Miss Henderson again, then I'm afraid you're wasting your time."

"And ours," Lang said.

Patrick wanted to punch Lang square in the jaw, but refrained from it; the thought of prison wasn't so appealing. "Like I said, I bought her house at auction earlier this year. Everything was fine until I got a visit from a Sam Leonard only a few days ago, telling me he thinks he's being haunted by her."

Preston frowned.

"He's her ex-partner; we questioned him about her death. He knew nothing about it."

"He didn't know anything. Sam came to me for help, and by pure coincidence, it turned out I had bought his ex-girlfriend's house. I made connections with other members of the Henderson family."

"Dead, I assume?" Lang interrupted, with sarcasm.

"Yes, actually, there's a book of family archives in my loft. The house has a lot of history to it, and the family were very wealthy. Zoe was the last surviving Henderson. Anyway, as I was saying, I made a connection with one. Her name was Anna. She made me aware Zoe was murdered."

Lang got up from his seat and walked to the whiteboard. "You see this here, Patrick?" He pointed to a picture of a young girl's face. "This here is a murder enquiry and involves one dead girl and a loose killer. This is what's real, not your silly little ghost stories. So, if you don't mind…"

Preston stood up. "He's right, Patrick, we can't do this anymore. You had the chance to work with us, and you turned it down. We did our job; this set up," his hands flapped back and forth between himself and Patrick, "it's dead and buried. Sorry, mate. There's nothing we can do."

Patrick got up, feeling defeated. He made a last attempt. "There's one more thing. Sam gave me a photograph, and there's something about it I can't quite put my finger on. I was wondering if you could have a look."

Preston shook his head. "Right, what is it?"

"A photo of Sam and his new girlfriend, Deborah. The frame was damaged by an unknown force this morning. Sam said he witnessed it himself."

Lang rolled his eyes.

Patrick produced the photo, and as he was about to hand it to Preston, he felt it pulled from his grasp.

"Did you not hear me the first time?" Lang said as he looked down at the picture. He fell silent as his eyes set on the people in the picture.

"What is it, Jim?" Preston asked as he saw Lang's expression change.

For once, Patrick was still unsure what was going on. He knew there was something about that picture but could not place what it was.

"What did you say her name was?" Lang asked quietly.

"Deborah. Her name is Deborah Bell."

Lang looked up and met Preston's eyes. "That girl's name is not Deborah Bell," he said as he handed the photo to Preston.

"What?" Patrick asked in confusion.

Preston took the picture from Lang's hands and looked down at the faces. His stomach lurched, and his face became pale.

"What's wrong?" Patrick asked.

Preston couldn't find his voice; his lips had gone dry. After what seemed like an eternity of silence, he finally uttered the words which changed everything. "Jim's right. Her name isn't Deborah Bell. Her name is Jane. Jane Preston. That's my daughter."

Patrick frowned. Was he hearing this right? "Are you sure?"

"Of course he's bloody sure. You think he wouldn't know his own daughter?"

Preston sat down on his chair. "Why is she going by a different name? And how does she know the ex-boyfriend of Zoe Henderson?"

The three men fell silent in the office. What now?

35

Patrick had called Sam and asked him to attend the station to meet with Preston and Lang. Preston was still very confused about the photograph which pictured his daughter, Jane, with Sam Leonard, even though Patrick had informed him Sam had referred to her as Deborah Bell. There had to be some sort of mistake, surely. Preston had sent Lang away to see his doctor, since he had been complaining about the persistent headaches, and so Preston was alone in the office when Sam had appeared. Patrick sat down beside Sam, across from Preston, and at that moment, he had never wanted his colleague by his side more. He and Lang had a strong relationship, and even though they could be snappy with each other, they had become the best of friends over the years. Their families had come together for dinner parties and social gatherings, and Preston couldn't imagine what his life in the force would have been like had Lang not been a part of it. Lang had felt the same way and looked at Preston like a brother. It never did affect their work, though; when something needed done, it would be done properly and with precision.

"Paul, Sam's here to explain everything," Patrick said quietly.

Patrick had gone outside to meet Sam and had not explained in full why he had been called in. Sam understood he was to explain why he thought Zoe's death was not accidental; however, Patrick was slowly piecing together how this assumption had come to be.

Preston stood up and shook Sam's hand. "We meet again," was all he could manage.

"Has Patrick explained everything about my flat and his house?" Sam asked.

Preston nodded as they all sat down.

"So, you think we could be right?" Sam asked. "You think Zoe may have been killed intentionally?"

Preston ignored the question. "The photograph that Patrick brought in." He slid open his drawer and lifted out the frame. "Can you tell me who this is in the picture with you?"

Sam looked at Patrick and frowned. "Deborah. She's my girlfriend."

"Deborah, you say?"

Sam nodded, unsure as to where the conversation was headed but with a gut feeling it was not going in the right direction.

"Deborah...?"

"Bell," Sam drew out the surname slowly.

Preston turned the frame to face him and looked down at his daughter's face.

Patrick had gone into a minor daze and could see how this was going to pan out. He knew what was about to happen would end Preston, and his career.

"You see, Sam, the woman in this picture is not called Deborah Bell. Her name's Jane, Jane Preston; my daughter."

Sam dipped his head forward slightly and laughed. "You can't be serious? I'm trying to figure out if I'm being haunted by my ex, who may have been murdered, and you're pulling tricks like that?"

Preston remained sullen faced. This was not the kind of joke that would make him laugh, or even crack a smile. "No joke, Sam. This *is* my daughter. Jane."

Sam looked at Patrick for support. Patrick shook his head. Sam got up quickly from his chair. How could this be happening? "Forgive me for being a tad slow on the subject, but you say her name's Jane?"

Preston nodded again, beginning to understand the potential horror that could be about to tear his family apart.

"But Deborah and I have been together for close to a year, give or take a few weeks. I would've known if she was lying."

Preston shook his head. "And did you know Jane and Zoe Henderson were best friends before Zoe died? She and my other daughter were devastated when they found out what had happened to her."

Patrick had been quiet to allow Sam and Preston the time to unravel the mystery of what had been going on. He heard the handle on the office door turn, and he spun around slowly on his chair to find Lang peep his head in. Patrick got up and went outside.

"You're back quick," Preston said. "Everything okay?"

"Never mind that, what's going on?" Lang pushed Patrick aside and went into the office.

When he sat down and listened to the conversation, he was astounded by the revelations. "Am I hearing this right?" Lang asked.

Preston was angrier than he had ever been. But he wasn't sure who he was angry with. He could not believe what Preston's daughter had been doing, and he was angrier he hadn't seen it.

Sam was slumped on the chair in front of Preston and felt like he had been knocked over by a truck. He had been living a lie for the past year. He had been dating someone who wasn't real, someone who had lied and betrayed his trust. "Why would she pretend to be someone else?" Sam asked.

Patrick had been quiet for long enough. "Paul, I'm sorry to say this, but I think you need to get Jane in for questioning about the death of Zoe Henderson."

Preston didn't want to admit it, but Patrick was right. Everything that had been said over the past half hour led them to believe Jane knew more about Zoe's death than she had first let on, one way or another.

"Paul, you know you can't be the one to deal with this. It'll have to be me or passed on to another team." Lang's voice echoed in Preston's ears.

Preston nodded in disbelief. His life had just changed in a single moment.

"You continue to work on the Prowse case, and until I can get someone to deal with this, I'll take it on. You okay with that?"

"Aye."

Lang led Sam into another room. He walked down the corridor, massaging his temples in rhythm with his walk. He was not prepared to let his health issues get in the way of work, not after what had happened. Preston needed him now more than ever, and he could not let him down with his own problems. He would tell him when the time was right.

Sam stood beside the table in an interview room, and his mind was going crazy. He felt like he was in one of his plays, like this wasn't really happening.

"Sam, we need you to talk to Jane."

Sam nodded. "It feels so strange when you say Jane." His eyes began to fill. "I've known her as Deborah the whole time. How could she do this?"

Lang shook his head. "How do you think it feels for DS Preston back there? He's in bits, and we need you to help us fix this."

Sam felt sick. "How can any of this be fixed?"

Lang sat down at the table and gestured for Sam to sit down too. The room matched Sam's mood: cold and gloomy.

"I'm going to need you to phone Jane, arrange to meet her. Try to get the truth out of her."

Sam wondered how it could be possible. "I'm not so sure I can do this."

Lang bit his bottom lip and shook his head. "You don't have much of a choice, son."

36

I sauntered around the shops on Buchanan Street, and for the first time in a long time, I actually felt normal. No one knew who I was or what I had done, and certainly no one cared. I looked at the people around me, going about their business with loved ones or on their own, and I felt safe. I thought about going back home to Sam after my shopping trip (even though I had not actually purchased anything), and it made me smile. I could not stop smiling. I looked in the shop windows, and I looked up at the cloudy, bleak sky over Glasgow. It didn't alter my mood that was for sure. I felt my mobile vibrating in my jacket pocket, and I took it out to see Sam's name lighting up the screen. I smiled once again.

"Hey, babe, what's up?"

"Can you come back to the flat?"

Something was wrong. His voice sounded flat. It made my stomach flutter and not in a good way.

"What's wrong?"

"Nothing, I just want to ask you something."

He sounded odd. The kind of odd when you know something bad has or is going to happen, and you know it's out of your control.

"So, ask away. I'm on a shopping trip. You can't ask a girl to interrupt a shopping trip, can you?" My attempt at humour failed.

"Just come back to the flat as soon as you can, please."

The line went dead.

I began to panic, my skin tingled, and my heart pounded. My stomach felt like it was twisting inside to the point where it was going into cramps, and I could feel tears sting my eyes.

That's it, I thought. *He's had enough and wants to end it.*

I supposed I knew that this day would come eventually; I mean, how could I spend the rest of my life with him when I was living a lie? I turned and made my way back down Buchanan Street and turned left onto Argyle Street. As I walked past people in the street, I felt like I was being watched. Every set of eyes I made contact with bore into me like some sort of demon. Then, I realised every set of eyes I looked into were Zoe's eyes. She was everywhere, and in daylight. It was like she was there, right in front of me, as alive as I was.

Of course, I knew it was ridiculous, but the more I tried to block it out, the more I saw her. Then, the low hum of conversations all around me turned to one voice, with one word being said over and over.

Murderer!

I tried to be strong. I tried to show I was not scared of her tormenting. It was then I saw the other one. Claire Prowse. I didn't see her the way I saw Zoe; I saw Claire the way she was the last time I saw her, lying on the ground with a stab wound to the neck. She was on every corner, every shop doorway. The street was littered with the vision of her death.

I put my head down and walked faster than my legs could carry me. Without looking up, I found my way back to Sam's flat and climbed the stairs slowly, slower than usual, to try to compose myself. My time with Sam was about to end, and I was not so sure how I would react. I honestly didn't know if I would simply allow him to end things, and I could go back to being myself, Jane. I was sure I would not be able to carry on living without him. The thought of life without Sam suffocated me.

I put the key in the door quietly and went inside. The place was silent, eerily silent. "Hi!" I called out as cheerfully as I could.

"I'm in the kitchen." His voice was what I could only describe as dead, like his feeling for me had become I could only presume.

I walked into the kitchen and stood in the doorway, my bag swinging by my side, and my stomach cramping so much I thought I would vomit right there on the kitchen floor.

"What's all the hurry to get me back?" I said, failing to hide the shakiness in my voice.

Sam's eyes were red, not from tears but from anger. I had never seen him look so mad. It scared me a little. "Why haven't I met your family yet?"

What? I thought. *What an odd way to initiate a breakup.* "Excuse me?"

"I mean, we've been together for a long time now. You've met what little family I have. Why haven't I been introduced to yours?" His eyes blazed.

"I told you, my family aren't that nice. We have a history and not a good one. I don't want to spend any time with them, and I certainly don't want you to have to either."

Sam shook his head. "So, your sister Lisa… you don't get along with her?"

The vomit rose so quickly it startled me, but I managed to keep it down. *How the hell does he know about Lisa?*

"I don't have a sister called Lisa. Where did you get that from?" My hands were sweating, and my stomach was so sore it was travelling down to my thighs.

"Don't lie to me. I know." He stood up and walked over to me, with a look on his face which made me realise this was not just a breakup. He knew; he knew everything.

"You know what?"

He grabbed my chin and jolted my head up so I could look him dead in the eye. "You know *exactly* what I'm talking about, Deborah."

I pulled away from him, shocked at his aggression. I was speechless; I never knew he had it in him to be so brutal.

"Or do you prefer Jane?"

It was then whatever strength I had left had disappeared and been replaced by blind fear. I ran out of the flat and didn't look behind me.

37

I found myself staring up at the house where it all began: my other life. The life which I thought I was able to control, the life which I believed I could create and be happy. It turned out to be something which at first was incredible — I had never felt love like it in my life, and, to be honest, before Sam, I never really believed such love existed. He made me feel more alive than I had ever felt before. He made my heart beat to the point where I thought I would explode. Truth be told, I would have taken a bullet for that man; I would die for him. When we first came face to face, I could never have imagined getting to this point. In actual fact, it was never meant to get this far. Had I been honest from the beginning, things may well have been different.

Knowing he had discovered my secret changed things. He looked at me with disgust when he called me Jane. How had he found out? How could he know without me being the one who told him?

Of course, I figured out that it had to be the psychic. Ironic, really, considering I believed them to be the biggest liars ever to have walked the planet. He was the only person I could think of, and with everything that had happened in Sam's flat, it had to be the only explanation. My real name kept ringing in my ear with Sam's voice behind it. I never thought I would hear him call me Jane.

As I looked up at Henderson Manor, I wondered if this Patrick would be inside. I found myself knocking on the door, and for a split second, bile had risen to my throat as I imagined Zoe answering the door. Of course, she did not.

My knuckles made contact with the thick wooden door, and I heard the sound echo behind it. The early signs of winter were beginning as I looked up at the sky and saw the stars twinkle. It was so cold, and I could hear the gravel crunch beneath my feet. I believed it to be possible if I ever saw Sam again, it would be my last time. I could feel it in the air and in my blood.

I heard footsteps approaching the front door, but I was surprised when it opened to see a female standing inside. She looked at me with uncertainty.

"Can I help?" She smiled gently.

I couldn't speak.

"Are you looking for someone?"

I nodded.

"Are you okay?" she asked.

I finally managed to find my voice. "I used to be friends with the girl who last lived here."

We both stood in silence for a few moments. I had no idea what I expected her to say. I had no idea who she even was.

"Why don't you come in?"

I stepped over the threshold and averted my eyes from the staircase. Something made me question my own sanity. But then, I was already able to answer my own question. I knew I had lost it, but nothing could stop my irrational behaviour when it came to Sam.

"It's always hard to lose someone. Were you both close?"

Why was she being so nice to a stranger? She had no idea who I was, and she had opened her door to me. She seemed so kind.

"I'm Jane," I said. My voice cracked.

"I'm Jodie." She held out her hand.

Something caught the corner of my eye, and I turned quickly to look.

"This is Lewis. He's a little rascal."

Shit! What the hell am I doing here, in this house? This isn't Zoe's house anymore. This is a family home, the psychic's family, the psychic who had wrecked my life.

"I bet he is," I said, with a smile.

The baby was strapped into a pram, and it was then I realised she was wearing a coat.

"Oh, I'm sorry, were you on your way out?"

"No, actually, we've just arrived. Long story, but we've been away for a while."

Probably would have been better for her if she had stayed away. If this Patrick character wanted to go messing up my life, then he would pay for it. I had killed in this house before, and I could certainly do it again if I had to.

"I should go; you've obviously got a lot on. I miss her, that's all."

Jodie shook her head. "Don't be silly. You came here for a reason. Stay for a cup of tea at least."

38

Patrick sat behind his desk in the church and wondered how his life had taken such a turn for the worst. Jodie had taken Lewis and left to stay with her parents until he was able to decide what was more important to him: his family or his work in the church. To say the last few years had proven difficult for them would be an understatement.

When Patrick had become involved with the triple murder case in Glasgow two years earlier, he could never have foreseen he would have had such a personal involvement. It almost tore them apart, and Jodie had almost died; hence the reason she had given up her place in the church and decided to close the door on that particular part of her life. Patrick, on the other hand, had still felt like he had so much to give and decided to continue his work with helping people in the church. It was not until Lewis came along that Patrick questioned his work and how it would affect his son; he continued with it all the same. When Sam turned up, Patrick knew he could not ignore him. When all was said and done, Patrick's house was directly involved in the situation.

Patrick filed away the last of the papers on his desk and ran his hand over the top of his head. "What the hell am I doing?" he said out loud.

Patrick picked up his phone and dialled Lang's number. "Jim, it's Patrick. Listen, I can't be a part of this anymore. It's ruining my marriage. I know you're probably quite thrilled by this."

"I can take it from here," Lang replied.

Patrick felt relief wash over him as he picked up his jacket and locked up the church. He made his decision there and then that

Jodie and Lewis would forever be his priority, and nothing would stand in their way. He was honest with himself when he realised this decision should have been made straight after Ross had died. There was nothing in the world Patrick wanted more than to protect his family from anything or anyone that could bring them potential harm. He looked down at his phone to see there was a text message from Jodie.

I'm at home whenever you're ready to talk. Lewis is excited to see his daddy. Love you. J x

Patrick smiled as he made his way across the street.

The area of Partick was still bustling with people and traffic, and as Patrick looked up Byres Road, he decided he would travel home by taxi. He flagged one down and gave his address. It had become dark, and the wind had picked up, and as the taxi was stationed at a set of traffic lights, Patrick could feel it swaying in the wind.

"They say there's a storm on the way," the driver said over the intercom.

"Aye, looks like it."

The driver was quiet again as they continued their journey, which Patrick was glad of; it would give him time to think about what he was going to say to his wife. He had no idea how he would explain himself and why it had taken him so long to decide his life with Jodie and Lewis was more important to him than the church and the dead. Before he knew it, the taxi was approaching the house.

"You want me to go up the drive, mate?"

"No, thank you. I'll walk from here."

Patrick paid the driver and walked up the drive. Lewis's bedroom was in darkness, and Patrick understood he was most likely to be asleep. Jodie was such a good mum and he would be eternally grateful for her commitment to their family.

Patrick approached the front door and realised it was open slightly; that wasn't like Jodie at all. "I'm home," he called out.

Jodie appeared from the living room door, and she had a mixture of emotions on her face. She hugged Patrick tight.

"I'm sorry for what I've put you through. I should've realised what I had to lose *well* before now. What made you come back? Is Lewis doing okay? Are you okay?" Patrick could not stop himself from talking. He was so glad to see his wife back in their home.

Jodie smiled at him. "I'm fine, Lewis is fine, and I came back because we're worth fighting for, don't you think?"

Patrick nodded.

"But before we go any further, I've something to tell you." Jodie said.

"Yes?"

Jodie smiled. "Someone's here."

Patrick looked through to the kitchen. "Who?"

"Someone who used to be friends with the girl who lived here before us. She was really upset when I answered the door so I let her come in for a bit."

Patrick's stomach flipped. "What do you mean you let her in?"

"She was upset. I couldn't shut the door in her face."

Patrick let go of Jodie and searched the kitchen and living room. Jodie frowned. "What on earth is wrong with you?"

"What did she say her name was?" Patrick whispered.

"Jane; and why are you whispering?"

Patrick gritted his teeth. "Where is she?"

"She's in the bathroom. What the hell is the matter?"

Patrick took his phone out to phone Lang.

"There's a strong possibility she *murdered* the girl who used to live here. She's been impersonating someone else for the last year or so, so she could form a relationship with Sam Leonard, the guy who came to me for help."

Jodie's eyes widened. "Are you serious?"

"Yes. Stay calm. I'm phoning Jim Lang. Keep her talking, and they'll be here within the next ten minutes. And don't let her know I'm here, if she doesn't already."

Jodie climbed the stairs, and Patrick went inside the living room to make the call.

"Jim, Jane Preston is here, in my house. You'd better get over here now, I think–" Patrick stopped when he heard Jodie's screams coming from upstairs. He dropped the phone and ran upstairs.

He found Jodie in Lewis's bedroom. He approached the cot and gripped the bar at the top. Lewis's yellow bear sat at the end of the mattress. Lewis was gone.

39

Lang had arrived at Henderson Manor around ten minutes after Patrick's phone call. He had stayed on the line after he had heard Jodie screaming and understood straight away what had happened. Lang had informed Preston, but no amount of reassurance from Lang could keep him and his family away.

"It's not a good idea for you to be involved now, Paul. You know this already," Lang had said. "I promise I will sort this, and everything will be okay."

Preston shook his head in disbelief. "How could she do this to us, Jim? How could she do it to them? I mean, that poor wee baby has been taken from his bed to God knows where."

Lisa Preston, along with her mum and grampa, were sitting in the back seat of the police car outside Henderson Manor. A uniformed officer was sat in the driving seat. Lang had gone inside with four uniformed officers and taken a statement from Jodie, who was worse than distraught.

"We'll do our best to find them, Jodie. I promise you that." Lang's voice was soothing, something Patrick had never seen in him before.

Outside the house, Lisa was trying to come to terms with what her sister was being accused of. "I can't believe that this is happening. I mean, Jane wouldn't harm anyone. Why all of a sudden is she being accused of murder and the kidnapping of a baby?"

Janet Preston wept silently as she stared out of the window, up at the house. A voice came through on the radio.

"We've had a call in of a possible suicide attempt on the Erskine Bridge south bound. Young child present at the scene, we request back up."

Inside the house, the radios on the officers' jackets sounded out, and the words echoed around the living room.

"It's her, I know it." Jodie became hysterical.

Lang felt bile rise to his throat. "Come on, we're going. All of us."

Jodie and Patrick followed Lang out to the cars in the drive and climbed into the one Lang was driving. Patrick wasn't surprised to see Sam in the back seat.

"Are you two okay? I heard what that officer said on the radio."

"No, I'm not fucking okay. That psycho bitch has stolen our baby boy and is hanging off the fucking Erskine Bridge with him," Jodie said.

Sam stayed silent.

"I think she knows the game is up. We'll get him back, baby. He'll be okay," Patrick said.

"I'm sorry," Sam replied.

"Jodie, this is Sam, the guy who I've been helping since you left. He's been fooled by Jane too. She's been living under another identity for the last year. She's suspected of murdering Zoe, the girl who lived here before us. Zoe used to be Sam's girlfriend."

Jodie did not reply. She turned her head to face out of the window, refusing to let the scream escape which had risen from her throat.

Lang rushed over to the car which was holding the Preston family.

"We're going now. If you insist on following, please don't get out of the car when we arrive. It will only encourage her to jump sooner."

Janet let out a sob in the back seat.

"I'm sorry, Paul, I really am." Lang jumped into his car, and the vehicles sped down the drive and into the street, sirens screaming along the way.

Turning onto Great Western Road and heading towards the Clydebank area, Auld Tam Preston had turned green with nausea.

"Paul, I need to tell you something," he said, trying to be heard over the sirens.

Preston turned to face him. "What is it, Dad?"

"The other day, when I was at your house, the day Barbara won at the bingo?"

"Aye, what about it, Dad?" Preston was distant. He worried his daughter would be dead by the time they reached the bridge.

"I tried tae log on to my Facebook on the computer, and I found a Facebook page already logged on. It was Jane's, but it wisnae her name. It was Deborah Bell, but oor Jane's face in the picture."

"It's okay, Grampa, you weren't to know." Lisa reached out and held his hands.

The car zigzagged in and out of the traffic at Anniesland Cross and sped through towards Knightswood.

"Aye, hen, I know that, but if I'd questioned her a wee bit more, then maybe that poor wee wean widnae be up on that bridge."

Paul Preston turned around and focused on the road ahead. The car past Knightswood and sped along Great Western Road, past Drumchapel and through the roundabout at Kilbowie Road. He watched the other police cars in front of them weave in and out of the traffic and couldn't believe that this time, they were on their way to the bridge to stop the attempted suicide of his daughter, who had kidnapped a baby.

"Paul?" Janet's voice penetrated his thoughts.

Preston slid his hand behind the seat, and Janet reached out to take his hand. "It's all right. She won't jump."

Lisa closed her eyes as the car flew down the boulevard, past the Ocean Field housing estate and down towards the bridge. The police cars in front slowed slightly, lights still flashing but sirens no longer providing a deafening ring to their ears. A police barrier had been set up at the entrance to the bridge, and the officers at the scene lifted the barrier to let the cars through.

Lang's voice came through the radio. "Paul, this is Jim. Do not, I repeat, do not get out of the car when we reach Jane's location. If she sees you, she might do something stupid."

Preston grabbed the radio. "So, what the fuck are we supposed to do?"

Lang's heart was breaking for his colleague and friend. "Let me do my job. You can trust me."

Preston knew Lang was right. He had to keep his family in the car; they could not risk Jane seeing them.

"We're going to let Sam talk her down. I'll be with him too."

"What about the baby?" Preston asked.

There was silence for what seemed like an eternity.

"Our priority is to get Lewis to safety."

Preston nodded and put the radio down.

Lisa and Janet were crying silent tears as Preston watched Lang's car approach Jane's position on the bridge. Jane Preston's daughter came into Preston's line of sight, and he wasn't prepared for what he saw. Jane had strapped little Lewis onto her back and was on the other side of the barrier. It was clear she had every intention of jumping. The Preston family froze in horror. Screams could be heard coming from the car in front.

Jodie McLaughlin watched as her son was dangled over the Clyde.

40

I looked across Glasgow as the lights twinkled and the wind grew stronger. It was cold on my face, and I knew the water would be even colder. I felt the pain in my thighs as I fought against the harsh elements to keep my stance on the bridge. The view was outstanding as I watched the lights across Glasgow. The River Clyde was almost directly beneath me, and I knew this was the best place to end everything. I wanted my last vision on earth to be a good one, and that's why I picked the Erskine Bridge.

My mum used to take me and my sister Lisa there in the summer at sunset, to let us see the beauty of Glasgow. It was a hard place to grow up sometimes, and she wanted to show us not everything in life had to be difficult, that we could make our lives sparkle, like Glasgow did up on that bridge at night. She had a way with words, our mum. And she was such a fantastic mum when we were growing up. She still was. So, what the hell had happened to me? When and why had I turned into such a monster? If this was what love did to people, then I didn't want it anymore. All I wanted was to be happy, and to make Sam happy. But he was not mine to begin with. Had I left things alone, everything would be fine.

Something to my left caught my eye, and I realised there were six police cars on the bridge. I saw one of the doors open, and my dad's colleague, Jim, got out of the driver side. I turned away. There was nothing he could do to stop me ending this horrific pain. I looked out at Glasgow and took a deep breath. Just as I was about to let go, I heard the sweetest sound you could ever wish to hear.

"Deborah…"

I turned to see my beautiful Sam, standing beside me, close enough I could reach out and touch him. I almost collapsed at the sound of his voice. I looked into his eyes to see they were blurry; he had been crying.

"Sam, what are you doing here?" I asked through sharp intakes of breath.

"Don't do this. We can fix everything."

I shook my head. He couldn't be serious, could he? "What do you mean we can fix everything? You know who I am, and what I've done. I'm a monster, and I can't deal with this right now. You need to leave."

My legs were shaking, and I didn't know if it was with fear or his presence. See what his presence did to me? My heart ached at the sight of his face, and my whole body went numb. They say love is a beautiful thing; I think love is evil.

"I'm not going anywhere until you come back over that railing and into my arms."

"You don't mean that."

Sam took a step closer. "Yes, I do."

He held out his hand. I wasn't sure I could trust him. With all the police here, I was certain he would hand me over to them.

"I can't."

My eyes stung with tears, and the wind battered my face. Then, I heard the sound of a baby crying. My eyes widened. I don't know how, but I had forgotten all about him.

"Let me take Lewis, I'll put him in the car with Lang, and then, you and I can go somewhere where no one can disturb us. We can talk about everything."

I shook my head. "Why would you want to talk to me after this?"

"Because," he said, as tears fell from his eyes, "you went to all those lengths to have me as your own, and you love me more than anyone has ever loved me. That has to count for something."

I was wary. Did he finally understand me? "But that psychic's ruined everything."

"Is that why you took the baby? Deborah, nothing is ruined. We'll be okay. I promise. But it will only be okay if you give Lewis to me."

I thought about what he had said. Was he being sincere? I hoped with all my heart that he was.

"Okay," I said.

Sam carefully lifted Lewis from the strap on my back. "I'll be back in ten seconds."

Sam ran over to Jim and handed the baby to him. I could hear the many sighs of relief as Sam handed the baby over. I turned to face out again. It was peaceful considering the circumstances, I had to admit. Perhaps giving Lewis back relaxed me a little more. I wasn't sure I would've jumped with him strapped to me. I just wanted that psychic to feel the way I had… did.

I felt a hand on mine again, a tight grip. I turned and was stunned to see my dad staring straight into my face.

"Dad… I'm sorry."

Never had I ever seen my dad cry until then. I looked over at the police cars on the bridge and could make out the psychic and his wife were cradling their baby. She was crying hysterically, and the psychic held them in his arms. Then, I saw my mum, sister, and Grampa Tam standing beside one of the cars, and they were all holding onto each other. My heart banged against my chest.

"What have I done, Dad?" My voice squeaked.

My dad took a deep breath, and the tears spilled over. "You're not very well, sweetheart. What you have done is very, very wrong, darling, but you're my little girl. I promise whatever happens that will not change, do you hear me?"

I nodded and looked across to Sam, who had climbed back into one of the police cars, and his gaze fell low, away from my eyes. He couldn't even look at me. I looked across at Lisa, who was sobbing.

"Jane, take hold of my hand, and I'll help you over. Come on."

Jane. I was torn between Jane and Deborah—my life then and my life now. My life would never be the way it was. Never.

"I love you, Dad. And Lisa and Mum and Grampa Tam."

My dad's grip tightened on my wrist as I held onto the barrier. "We know you do, sweetheart. Come on, over you come."

I twisted my body so I was facing my dad. Then, I let go. My dad didn't catch me.

As I fell, my dad's screams penetrated the rush of air in my ears as gravity took hold of my body. I was gone.

41

One Year Later

The 'for sale' sign was finally replaced with 'sold,' and Patrick and Jodie packed up the rest of their things. After Jane's death, they had both decided enough was enough. Patrick had decided he would take a step back from the church. Not completely but enough that he would be able to spend more time with his family. Patrick wanted to live life to the fullest with his wife and son, and did not want to think about death until he was faced with it himself as an elderly man.

Patrick had dealt with the courts and was able to have Zoe Henderson's body moved to her planned burial plot in the grounds of the manor.

"This house would never have been ours truly, Patrick," Jodie had said. "It would always have been Henderson Manor no matter what we did with the place. And with the burial plots outside, we would never have settled here."

"I know. It's a sad but nice history to the house. At least they're all together now."

Lewis was eighteen months old and an absolute rascal. They had decided to move into the cottage at Lomond Park for a while, to get some peace and tranquillity and plenty of safe space for Lewis to toddle around in. Patrick and Jodie would never regret their time as psychics, and they would always cherish the memories of helping others. But their time was to be spent bringing up their son, and Jodie wanted to be calm so nothing would happen during her second pregnancy.

"I'll carry the big boxes out to the van, and you get Lewis settled," Patrick said.

Jodie strapped Lewis into his car seat and looked up at Henderson Manor as Patrick put the last of the boxes into the back of the van.

"Do you think that a house can remember things?" Jodie asked.

"So much has happened in that house I would be surprised if it couldn't."

Patrick climbed into the driver's seat and started the van while Jodie took one last look over the manor. She looked up at the main bedroom window, and even though she was used to seeing spirits, was shocked to see the whole of the Henderson family at the large window. Jodie blinked a few times to be sure what she was seeing was truly there.

She found Patrick at her side, looking up too.

"Tell me you see that too," she said.

Patrick nodded.

The Henderson family, all of them including Zoe, smiled as Patrick and Jodie climbed into the van and drove down the gravel drive and onto the street.

Henderson Manor was finally at peace.

***

Janet Preston opened the door and welcomed Jim Lang into the house. Today was the day of Auld Tam's funeral, and Lang being not sure how Preston was coping, due to everything else that had happened.

"How is he?" Lang asked quietly.

"He's bearing up. He'll be glad to see you though."

Lang hugged Janet and walked into the living room. Preston was in the kitchen, staring into the back garden.

"You all right?" Lang asked.

"Aye, I'm not bad. How's the head?"

Lang had been diagnosed with a brain aneurysm just after Jane had died and had been told it was inoperable. "I'm still alive, if that's what you mean."

The two had been able to joke about it, but with the death of Auld Tam, it was difficult to make light of things.

"How do you find it?" Preston asked.

"Find what?"

"Not working on the force anymore."

Lang shrugged. "It's strange, I'll give you that. But it's nice spending time at home. You never know how long you have, eh?"

Preston nodded. "That's true."

Preston had decided to leave the police force after his discovery of Jane's secret life. His decision was made once CCTV footage had revealed Claire Prowse's murderer was in fact Jane. It had all been captured on a street camera, right beside the car park where Claire had been stabbed in the neck. Preston never ever understood why his daughter ended up the way she had. But it had changed his life and his family forever.

Janet walked into the kitchen. "The cars are here."

Preston looked at Lang. They had known each other long enough to know the meaning behind that particular look.

"I know, mate. It's going to be hard, but you'll get through it. I'm here for you buddy."

Lang put his hand on Preston's shoulder and walked out to the cars with Preston's family. Lang's wife, Mary, was outside waiting by their car.

"It's at times like this when you need your friends around. I'll see you at the cemetery," Lang said as Preston, Janet and Lisa got into the car.

Lang and Mary got into their car and followed the funeral procession to the cemetery.

"I don't know how much more that man can cope with, Mary, I really don't. That family has been ripped apart by their own daughter. It's at times like this you want your parents' support and he's about to cremate his dad."

Mary held onto Lang's hand. "I know, sweetheart. But that's why you're here."

"Aye, but how long have I got left?"

Mary sighed. "You've got many a year left in you, I'm sure. And if that time comes, if I'm still alive, he'll be there for me, like you've been there for him."

The women in Lang and Preston's lives were the strongest women they would ever know. Janet and Mary had been the rocks of each family. Lang had worried about everyone other than himself once he had been given his terminal diagnosis. He had had a good life and had felt like he had made, if anything, a small difference in the city of Glasgow. He hoped that whoever took over from his and Preston's post in the force that they would continue to make a difference to the city. Their time in the force was just a memory, and Lang wondered for how long he would be able to conjure up those memories before his tumour would no longer allow it.

***

After the service, Preston disappeared from the crematorium and made his way out to see Jane. He walked slowly as he approached her gravestone and a single tear dropped from his eye.

"Why did this have to happen to my family?" Preston dropped to his knees and wept like a baby. He felt a strong hand fall upon his shoulder, and Preston attempted composure.

"Come on, mate. Let's have a whisky in Auld Tam's honour," Lang said as he put his arm around Preston and helped his best friend back to the car.

***

Jenny got out of bed and picked up the post from the doormat. She searched through it quickly in the hope there was a letter from Sam. When she saw the envelope and recognised the handwriting, her heart ached. She missed her friend so dearly. After the 'Deborah' situation, Sam had not been coping and had been turning down work. He had decided to leave and go to Australia for a year. His year was almost over, and even though Jenny knew it was selfish, she was excited he would be coming home soon.

She ripped open the envelope and pulled out the letter. As she read it, tears filled her eyes.

Dear Jenny,

How are you? My time in Oz is almost over and the thought of going back to Scotland is making me feel sick. I'm still seriously messed up, so I've decided to go to America for a while. Some friends I've met here have offered for me to stay with friends of theirs in Washington, and so I've taken them up on their offer. I would love it if you'd come out to join me.

I miss you Jenny, but I can't come home. Every time I think about it, I see her face and I can't bear it. I hope that you'll understand.

Lots of love,

Sam

Jenny put the letter in her pocket and went into the kitchen and switched on the kettle. The flat was so empty and quiet without Sam. Jenny knew he would never come home.

The flat would be empty and quiet forever.

Epilogue

The whisky flowed, the wine was poured and the dinner was served. Zoe Henderson was in awe of what was happening around her. If this was death, then she didn't mind it so much.

"The roast is perfect for a family reunion," Edith Henderson said as she placed the food on the large dining table.

"Are you all right, dear?" Helen Henderson asked Zoe.

Zoe could only nod.

"We've waited on you for a long time, Zoe. You must understand that," George Henderson said.

Zoe looked around the dining table at her whole family, ancestors and all. Henderson Manor was filled with every Henderson she had ever known of. She turned to her left and found her mother, Audrey, sitting next to her. She smiled sweetly at her daughter and couldn't believe everything that had happened in… how long had it been? She couldn't be certain, but what Zoe was certain of was Patrick McLaughlin had found justice for her, and that was all she had ever wanted. He had somehow managed to have her body moved to its proper resting place: at Henderson Manor. Now, she found herself, in spirit, sitting around the dining table with the rest of her family.

"I can't quite believe how this is actually happening, but I couldn't be happier that it is. I never thought this was possible."

As the conversation continued into the small hours, Zoe excused herself from the table and made her way out to the hall where she had met her death. She remembered how she had died and tried not to allow Jane Preston's memory to flood her mind.

Audrey came to Zoe's side, looking down at her daughter's place of death. "I would certainly assure you wanted more for you in life than you had. It couldn't have been nice to have had to deal with what you did. I was with you the whole time."

Zoe smiled. "I'm glad I'm here. If this is death, then it's not as scary as I thought it would be."

The happy family sounds from the kitchen made Zoe feel at peace forever.

***

The little girl had wandered off to explore the house. She'd gone into one of the rooms on the top floor and found an old yellow teddy bear. She lifted him high above her head and danced around the room with him. The little girl wanted to take him home.

"It's not fair that you're here all on your own. I'll take you home where you can play with my other bears. We can have a teddy bears picnic," she said as she continued to dance around.

He stays here, little one.

The girl stopped, her heart began to pound in her chest. "Hello?" Her voice was merely a whisper. She was quiet for a moment, holding her breath as she listened out for the person who spoke. When she was sure she'd imagined it, she made for the door, clutching the yellow bear at her chest.

He stays here. The voice was firmer this time. She couldn't make out if it was a man or a woman. In fact, she didn't know if it was more than one person. It sounded odd. It sounded irritated. She turned to face the window. An old woman was sat in a rocking chair. She was smiling at the little girl.

The girl dropped the bear and ran down the stairs, meeting her parents at the bottom.

"What do you think, Meela? Would you like to live here?" her mother asked.

She shook her head furiously. "No, I don't like it."

The family made their way outside and the estate agent followed them. He closed the door of Henderson Manor with a deflated expression on his face. "You're sure you don't want to think about it a little more?" he said to the family.

The woman looked down at her daughter and then to her husband. "I'm sorry, if my daughter doesn't like it, then we're not buying."

The estate agent tried not to show disappointment, even though every family who had ever viewed Henderson Manor seemed enthusiastic at first, and then, by the end of the viewing, said that they were no longer interested. Most of those families had young children. "Okay, what about the other properties we talked about?"

They walked slowly down the gravel driveway, the sound of the voice droning in the little girl's ears as she looked up at Henderson Manor. An old woman waved at her and smiled before she was surrounded by several more people, all of different ages. They all wore very different clothing to the types of clothes the she saw her parents and even her grandparents wear. The oldest woman, whom the little girl had seen sitting in a rocking chair, was standing at a separate window and was also waving. She was holding the yellow teddy bear.

She continued to stare up as the old people faded away from window. The little girl ran down the gravel driveway after her parents, too scared to look back in case the woman was following her.

The house would never belong to anyone else, it would always remain as it was, as it always had been: Henderson Manor.

Acknowledgements

Thank you to all at Bloodhound Books, to my editor who really helped me to delve deeper into my work and make it the best version of itself, family and friends, bloggers and readers.

A special thanks goes to Noelle Holten, a reader and a friend.

Thank you to my husband, Chris, who listens to all my initial ideas and encourages me to put them on paper.

www.ingramcontent.com/pod-product-compliance
Lightning Source LLC
Chambersburg PA
CBHW032212190626
46810CB00019B/2731